The
Boy
Who
Couldn't

R Coverdale

First published 2019 by Willow Breeze Publishing
Copyright © 2019 R Coverdale
The right of R Coverdale to be identified as the author of
this work has been asserted by her in accordance with
the Copyright, Designs and Patents Act 1988.

Cover design by Amanda at Let's Get Booked
Internal Illustrations copyright Michael Douglas Carr

ISBN: 978-1-9161080-1-1

A CIP catalogue record for this book is available from
the British Library.

DEDICATION

This book is dedicated to my dad, who gave me my love of nature and my mum, who gave me my love of books.

ACKNOWLEDGMENTS

Thank you to my long-suffering husband who believed in me *after* he read the first draft. "I didn't realise you had talent!" Thanks also to my children who have allowed me to bore them to death about the book. Further thanks to my lovely Labrador Toby who lies at my feet whenever I'm typing and was the inspiration for the dog in the story. Thank you to the numerous badger enthusiasts and groups all over the internet and the wonderful librarians who have been a constant source of information about badgers. Thank you to all the troubled children I've met over the years who gave me the inspiration for Greg, I truly hope you find the peace you deserve. Thanks go to Amanda at Let's Get Booked who kindly read and edited my novel. Ruth Mallon and Janine Cobain, my absolutely wonderful beta readers. Thanks also to a variety of friends and friends' children who proof read the story. Huge thanks to Craig Fellowes of The Badger Trust who approved all the badger and police facts and who's enthusiasm reignited the project when I had become jaded. Thank you to my various friends in the police whose advice helped me to help Greg avoid too much trouble. And thank you to you for reading this story. Without readers, stories are never born, they're just a huge jumble of letters on an old, dead tree.

CHAPTER 1

* JAMES *

How had this happened? How had my life come to this?

Never before had I realised how frightening real-life could be. I'd read books and watched films about criminals, but they were all make-believe – fiction. Suddenly I was in the middle of a real-life drama, and I was terrified.

I lay there among the tools and rubbish and began to sob. Just a few months earlier, my life had been perfect...

*   *   *   *   *

It was a beautiful summer morning as I sneaked into my parents' room. Their alarm clock warned me that it was 5:05am, but I took no notice. This was going to be the best day of my life so far. It was my birthday. My mum's sleepy eyes smiled at me and her warm arm collapsed around me as I snuggled in next to her.

A whole minute later, I couldn't stay still any longer. "*Please* get up," I begged.

"Okay," she half groaned, half smiled as she forced herself up. She nudged my dad. "Come on sleepy head, you're not getting away with it."

Outside, birds were chirruping loudly, Dad said they were joining in with my birthday celebrations. Mum fetched my baby sister, Rosie to witness the great occasion of my eleventh birthday and we all went downstairs together.

I slowly opened the living room door to reveal a shiny mountain of elegantly wrapped presents. I stood there, admiring my mountain from top to bottom and back up again. Carefully, I reached up and removed the top one first. It was the smallest of all the presents but somehow it was the most exciting with its scarlet rosette dramatically placed on top. I undid the red ribbon and removed the sticky tape. "Just rip it open!" shouted my dad who couldn't bear the way Mum and I had to unwrap presents so carefully, saving the paper and decorations for another time. I unwrapped it even slower and Mum winked at me as dad sighed in despair. Inside was... a bicycle bell?

"Thanks," I smiled, puzzled, "But I don't have a bike." I looked back at the pile of presents as though a bike shaped gift would suddenly appear where I hadn't noticed one before. I looked at Dad. Dad looked at Mum. Mum looked at Rosie. Rosie burped.

"Well, you'll just have to pretend won't you

then," said Dad. "Fancy a cuppa, Mum?" he asked as he turned and headed towards the kitchen.

I was beginning to unwrap the next present when Dad returned. "Ta daaa," he grinned as he wobbled into the living room on a shiny red bike. I just stood there. I knew I had a stupid grin on my face but I couldn't help it. *Flash!* Mum had taken a picture of me with my stupid grin – oh great.

"Oh Mum, Dad, thank you! Are you sure you can afford it?" Even though I'd hoped, I just couldn't believe it. We weren't rich any more like we used to be and I didn't think we'd be able to afford a brand-new bike.

"Don't be daft. We might not have as much money as we used to, but we're still okay," Mum reassured me.

Until recently, we had lived in a spacious four bedroomed house in the small market town of Inglehow. Mum and Dad both worked full-time and my little one-year-old sister Rosie and I were cared for by our childminder.

I remember the look on Dad's face when he came home early from work that dreadful day. Mum and Rosie and I were sitting at the table eating Chinese take-away. Dad came in and he didn't need to say a word. "What's happened?" my mum asked, getting up from the table.

"I don't have a job," he said, staring into space. "I can't believe it. I don't have a job. The receivers came in and..."

I didn't know what 'receivers' were but I knew it was serious. Rosie and I just sat staring as Mum hugged Dad and Dad hugged Mum. Rosie began crying. Even though she was too young to understand, she'd picked up on the atmosphere, she was sensitive like that.

Over the next few weeks, there followed lots of hushed conversations behind closed doors. Lots of false smiles and hidden tears. Then one morning, Mum and Dad summoned me into the living room. They were perched on the edge of the sofa, sitting stiffly upright as if they were in a business meeting. "Sit down," they instructed. "We've decided that you are old enough to be told what *has* happened and what *will* happen."

They explained that when they'd both been working, they'd had enough money coming in and had been able to afford our life of luxury. We went on holiday every year, had two nice cars, I went to scouts, piano lessons and karate, and Rosie's childminder took her to swimming club and toddler groups during the day when I was at school. "We've always been what we've called comfortable," Mum explained. "Not rich like film stars, not multi-millionaires, but we've always had enough money, so we've never needed to worry about finances."

"However, we haven't really been *rich* in the ways that matter," Dad continued. "Mum and I have been working such long hours that we haven't managed to spend enough time with you two or each other."

"We've decided to enrich our lives a different way. Dad's not going to look for work, he's going to be a 'stay-at-home-dad.'"

"What's one of those?"

"It means literally, that I am going to stay at

home and be a full-time dad to you and Rosie." A grin spread across his face. "We'll need to make some cut backs, we'll be moving into a smaller house and selling a car as we'll only need one. Our holidays will be staycations instead of trips abroad and we won't need a childminder to look after the pair of you, I can do it all. I'll take you to school and take Rosie to the park. I'll do the shopping, the cooking, the cleaning –"

"But Mum does the cooking."

"Not all of it she doesn't, I help out wherever I can, and I'll soon become a good cook. This is a great opportunity, it means I can spend more time with you and Rosie, you don't need to go to the childminders..."

"But I like going to the childminders."

This was not at all what I expected. I liked my life and I didn't want it to change. Judy, our childminder, was always happy and never ran out of fun ideas to do after school. I loved my dad, but he was often short-tempered and grumpy. I didn't think swapping fun activities with Judy for time with a grumpy dad was a good deal at all. I said as much and stomped up to my room, slamming doors behind me.

Later, when I came back downstairs, Dad had gone out and Mum was reading Rosie her favourite story. I knew I had been mean and I felt ashamed, but I still didn't like the idea that our life was about to change. Rosie gurgled at me and I tried to smile back at her.

Mum placed Rosie and the book down on the floor and pulled me towards her for a hug. "You know love, one of the reasons Dad can be grumpy is because he works too hard. Give him a chance, he doesn't like 'Grumpy Dad' much either."

So there it was. The decision had been made. Dad's posh car was sold and Judy held a little leaving party for Rosie and me. We sold our big town house and rented a cramped cottage on my uncle's farm.

My friend Ahmed was jealous of me. He didn't understand, because his dad wasn't like mine. Whenever *his* dad was home on leave, he was always doing fun things like taking Ahmed and his big brother out on mountain bike rides or taking them to the local car track.

"If my dad didn't have to go away to work, we'd be having fun twenty-four-seven," Ahmed beamed. "You're so lucky." I didn't want to tell him that my dad never does those things, so I just smiled back.

The first advantage I discovered about having a stay-at-home-dad was that I could ride my bike to school instead of travelling in a car. The second advantage I discovered was that my dad's after-school-hot-chocolates are the best thing I have ever tasted. Complete with marshmallows, squirty cream and sprinkles, yum! It was a good job his hot chocolates were so good – something had to make up for the splodge he presented us with at tea time. I complained loudly and begged mum to take back the cooking, but they both laughed and didn't take my request seriously. However, I didn't complain that as soon as Mum came home from work, she plonked herself down on the sofa and helped me with a jigsaw, or read Rosie a story. It was lovely having her spend so much time with us, and apart from occasional panicked cries from the kitchen, which would cause her to leave for a moment or two, we had more cosy time together.

Dad mastered five recipes, so we had the same five meals Monday to Friday, then mum cooked us special treats on the weekend.

The weekends were the biggest change. Mum and Dad used to rush around trying to do housework and fit in appointments they couldn't get to during the week. Now it was far more relaxed. We went out for day trips to the beach, walks through the woods, visited our cousins on the farm or just relaxed at home playing board games, watching films, and reading books. But the best change of all was in Dad. He was like a different person, not just happy, but *excited*. He loved hearing what I'd done at school and would tell me everything Rosie had done that day. Dad enjoyed pampering Mum and Mum enjoyed being pampered by Dad. All in all, it seemed that change wasn't such a bad thing after all.

And then the bullying started.

At first, I didn't realise I was being bullied. The bigger kids at school kept asking me what my dad did for a living and I proudly replied, "He's a stay-at-home-dad."

Then when they saw him waiting in the playground, they'd ask where my mum was.

"At work," I'd reply, confused why they were taking such an interest. Nobody had asked where my mum was when Judy used to collect me. Other dads collected, some were shift workers and some were unemployed. Nobody questioned them, so why was my dad so different?

"Your dad's a puff," I was reliably informed by a boy whose name I didn't even know.

"No he's *not*," I cried.

"And you are too, *cry*-baby."

And that was the beginning. I didn't tell Dad what they were saying at school. I still felt ashamed about the way I'd treated him when I found out he was going to be a stay-at-home-dad. I didn't want to hurt his feelings further by telling him the cruel things the bullies at school were saying.

The worst of them all was Grotty Greg. He was two years older than me and walked over from the secondary school each afternoon to collect his little brother. I didn't even know that he knew my name, but I knew his. He was feared by everyone.

I remember a couple of years ago when he went to our school and his mum used to collect him. The girls in my class always thought she was cool, with her perfectly groomed long blonde hair, designer clothes, and expensive jewellery. Her nails and handbags were always the same colour. That fascinated me – why would she feel the need to make them match? There was something about her though, she always seemed sad to me. When she smiled, it never reached her eyes.

Her son Greg was nothing like his mum. He had broad, powerful shoulders, wild ginger hair, and so many freckles on his face you could start to get dizzy if you dared to stare long enough. He was already nearly as tall as his mum and he spoke to her as though she was his slave.

"Idiot!" I remember hearing him call her once, when she realised she didn't have his trip money. I was shocked. I braced myself, waiting for her to tell him off, but she just turned and scurried home to collect it.

I remember telling my mum about it. "I can't believe she let him speak like that," I told her.

Mum looked sad. "Julie wasn't always like that," she sighed.

CHAPTER 2

* GREG *

It was me thirteenth birthday. As I ripped open me presents, I couldn't wait to get to the one I knew would be the latest X-Box game. Birthdays always meant mega party-time in our house, with loads of cousins, aunties, and uncles coming over with presents and staying to get smashed.

Dad loves to tell the story of me birth at every party – according to him, I nearly died as I was being born and according to him, if he hadn't dragged a doctor kicking and screaming into the room, I wouldn't be here today. Me dad always likes to tell the tale and it gets wilder and more exaggerated every time I hear it.

Dad played the new X-Box game with me in the living room, until there were too many people in the house and everyone was having to shout to be heard. I always liked these family parties, well... at the beginning I always did 'cos I got loads of presents.

After a while though, I seemed to be forgotten and the grown-ups would be having a better time than me, even if they did end up scrapping sometimes.

The black clouds in the sky looked like it was threatening to rain, so instead of everyone being outside, they'd all crushed into our living room. I went into the kitchen to see me mam, and she looked at me with tears in her eyes. "You look like you're feeling left out," she sniffed, "but stay a bit longer before you go to the park. Your dad loves to show you off to everyone."

I did stay for a while, but I started to feel more and more wound up. I wanted to play me X-Box game, but everyone was in the way. I wanted to talk about cars with Uncle Kev, but people kept butting in and I couldn't hear owt he was saying anyway.

Not only was everyone shouting to each other, but some bright spark had put a CD on as well. Granny called in, stinking of fags and gin and sticking wet, granny-breath kisses on me cheeks. I started to feel trapped. I had to get out of there. I grabbed me coat and ran.

By the time I reached the park me belly was in a knot and every muscle was tensed up. Me heart was beating like a big drum, real loud in me ears. I could feel pressure building in me throat as though I needed to scream or I would explode. I imagined me skull firing in all directions like nails from a bomb. I needed to hit out at sommat. Sommat or someone. And that someone was walking straight towards me.

He irritated me as soon as I saw him, with his floppy blond hair and his coat that was too big for his scrawny body. At the last minute, he looked up at me with his pathetic baby blue eyes and I hit him hard, right in the middle of his face.

If I hadn't been so angry, his look of shock as me fist swung towards him might've made me laugh. He fell straight to the floor and I stuck the boot in. A few hard kicks to his belly knocked all the wind out of him, and he couldn't even cry. I felt bad straight away, but it was too late. I'd done it again. I started to run.

Every time I got angry I hit out, and it was getting me into a load of trouble at school. Me dad used to be proper proud of me when I was younger and I'd got into scraps.

I was always big for me age. I felt tough. If I needed to hit someone or shove their face into the ground, I would, but half the time me reputation was enough to frighten them. Sometimes I did feel a bit bad for the kids I pushed around, but me antics gave me mates a good laugh, and me dad was always real proud of me being a tough kid. I learned not to care about me victims and just made sure everyone knew how much of a hard-case I was.

It was the same at home – I was hard like me dad. He was always showing Mam who was boss and I was always showing me kid brother who was boss.

"It's like this son, if yer don't show 'em who's boss they'll walk all over yer." Me dad used to warn me. Not that he liked me hitting me kid brother, but he'd just give me a clip round the ear and chuckle, "Wait 'til he's bigger than yer."

Little voices in me head would sometimes pop up and spoil the fun, make me feel guilty about being mean to me little brother, but I kept ignoring them.

I was dead proud of me dad. Even though he wasn't a tall man, he had this way about him that shouted *don't mess with me if yer know what's good for yer.* He had a big wide chest, "built like a brick out-house" me mates used to say. His nose had been flattened from too many fights and his broad forehead, looked even bigger 'cos of his shaved head. With his huge chest and arms from all his training sessions in the garage, only a nutter would be daft enough to fight him. He was covered with tonnes of tattoos, some of them home-made. The one on his right bicep was his favourite – his first fighting dog, Bronx. He was convinced it gave him the extra power he needed to spark someone out cold in a fight.

Dad was real proud of me reputation in the park and always laughed at the funny stories I'd tell him about winding people up and frightening them away. I wasn't like me little brother, who was an embarrassment to me dad. No, I was the favourite. I was the one me dad took to football. I was the one allowed to drink beer when his mates came round. He'd even said when I was old enough, I could come to the dog track with him.

But lately he didn't seem to take much notice of me. A couple of times when I'd told him about me fights, he actually told me to hold back a bit – he said as I get older the coppers can get hold of me and I've got to make sure I don't end up inside. Saying he didn't want me to end up like him. He said you rot away in prison. It made me wins seem worthless. That, and a teacher had told me she was sending me to a counsellor as though I had a problem. I told her there was nowt wrong with me and got real angry at her, calling her a nosey cow. She just shook her head and told me she was gunna send me anyway.

So would me dad be proud of me right now or angry? I didn't know, and that just added to me anger. I ran faster, pounding me feet into the ground. I thought about me mam too. Why did she have tears in her eyes when she asked me to stay? Why did she always seem to have tears in her eyes? Pathetic. If she's not happy then why doesn't she say sommat or do sommat? Even I noticed she was starting to live in the kitchen. The only times her and me dad spoke was to argue, and it was always her fault. Blubbing at him for this and for that and for the other. Why couldn't she just leave him alone? Or why didn't she just clear off out of the family instead of bringing everyone down? The more I thought about it, the angrier I got and the faster I ran until I realised I was out of town and in the woods.

I stopped and looked around, trying to work out where I was. I wasn't lost exactly, but I'd never been here before. It'd been raining at the park, but the rain seemed lighter here and couldn't get through at all in some places. I looked up and saw some leaves had turned brown for autumn but they were still hanging onto the trees. Clinging on like they didn't wanna let go.

Looking at the leaves more closely, I noticed that brown wasn't really the best way to describe them. They were all different colours, different shades of yellows, golds, and reds. I'd never noticed that before. They were covering the forest floor and there was sommat real calm about the way they muffled me footsteps. I felt... I dunno... safe. Like

I'd entered a real cosy room even though I was out in the wild.

Wherever I looked, all I could see was tree trunks, thin ones and thick ones, brown ones, green ones and silver ones. Above me head, the branches linked together making an arched roof like when we used to join hands for 'Oranges and Lemons' at nursery. There was sommat different about the smell too. It took a while for me to realise, but I couldn't smell traffic. I couldn't hear it neither. The knots in me belly had gone and I felt light, almost like I could float. I'd never felt anything like this before. I started to kick the leaves into the air and then watch them quietly fall back down and settle again. I kept kicking them and each time they drifted back to the floor I felt me heartbeat slowing down a bit more.

Just ahead, there seemed to be some kind of a path leading into the distance, so I followed it. I wasn't in no hurry and the path kept gently curving different ways so you couldn't see very far ahead. I felt hidden from the world. I just kept following it for ages and ages.

Eventually, I found an old iron bridge. This surprised me. I hadn't expected any humans to have ever been here. Probably none had been here in a long while 'cos the criss-cross patterned sides were looking rusty and the wooden walkway was covered in moss and had lost a few planks. Weeds were growing up through the gaps and over the railings so you couldn't even notice a bridge was there until you were almost on it. I don't know why a bridge had ever been built in the first place. The river it crossed was tiny. I could have jumped across the banks.

Standing on the bridge, I looked down at the leaves and twigs as they floated away. I felt the peace and quiet of the forest folding round me. As I stared at me reflection in the water, I felt meself being soothed into that feeling where you're awake but you can dream.

I remembered the days when Mam and Dad were nice to each other. When we used to sit and watch the TV together without me mam making excuses to be in the kitchen. I remembered when me dad was proud of me for sorting the posh kid from down the road. What would he make of me hitting that kid in the park today? Would he be proud or angry? I didn't know anymore. I wasn't proud. I wished I hadn't done it. Why had I done it?

I could feel meself getting wound up again, so I watched the leaves floating down the river, and straight away felt it calming me down again. The gentle burbling of the river as it trickled round rocks seemed to drown out any sound of real-life. I liked this place. I decided there and then that this was gunna be me very own secret place. A place I could disappear to and hide from everything. A place where nowt made me angry. There were no humans in me secret place.

Quietly, standing alone on me bridge, I realised I'd never stood so still and so quiet for so long before. I noticed a gentle tickling sensation on me skin spreading all over me body. It felt a bit like the beginning of pins and needles, but it just stayed real light. Me vision went a bit funny an all. I could see little bubbles in front of me like when you stand up too quickly and it makes your head spin. I still stayed where I was. I knew I should probably move but it was like I was in some kind of trance.

To me left, I heard a sudden scampering sound. I turned round to look and saw a squirrel leaping from place to place. I watched her for ages as she darted here and there, not bothered by me at all even though she saw me move position to watch her better.

As I wondered what she was doing, the funny bubbles in front of me eyes seemed to come together and a picture came into me head of a big pile of nuts and berries. I wondered if that was what she was doing – collecting nuts and berries for winter.

Suddenly, she froze and looked to her left. What had she seen? I froze to the spot. Me vision quickly cleared, but me head began to tingle. The squirrel was still, her eyes fixed on something. *What was it?*

I looked around and realised I was in the middle of nowhere, miles from anyone I knew. Owt could attack me and I mightn't be found for days. I could try to hide but if I moved, whatever it was might notice me. I could fight kids but what sort of kids would be in the woods? A crowd of country crazies maybe? Or what if it's a big wild animal?

I moved me eyes, searching for a weapon of sorts. Every big stick was part of a living tree. By the time I'd snapped it off, whatever it was would've already attacked me. What sort of wild animals live in the woods? Foxes? They're like dogs. I could maybe fight off one, but not a whole gang of them.

Me and the squirrel didn't move. We stayed like that for ages. It felt daft using the same defence as a tiny animal. And not a very good defence judging by the amount of dead squirrels I'd seen on the roads. One of us was gunna have to look. I could feel the hairs stand up on the back of me neck and the tingling in me head got worse as I forced meself to slowly, quietly, turn me head...

CHAPTER 3
* JAMES *

Due to the bullying and name calling, mostly instigated by Grotty Greg, I began to feel embarrassed about my dad picking me up from school. I wished he'd shave his head like some of the other dads to make him look tougher, but he was proud of what he called his 'thick mop'.

Dad's black hair was so thick and wiry it never seemed to do as it was told and stood up, pointing in all directions making him look like a mad scientist from a cartoon. His piercing blue eyes were such a contrast to his black hair and brown skin that people seeing him for the first time would look twice in surprise. All this, combined with his extreme height and thin build caused my dad to resemble a bright street lamp with a shaggy bird perching on top. He was extremely difficult to miss.

In an attempt to avoid drawing any more attention to him, I suggested he wait outside the playground for me to come out, instead of coming in

19

and standing with the mums. He agreed happily and said that would work better because then he could bring our dog Sam with him. I sighed with relief. I didn't want him to know he embarrassed me, but I was beginning to dread home-time and all the teasing that centred around his arrival.

The next day as I left the playground and walked towards Dad, I heard the unmistakable grind of Grotty Greg's voice shouting, "That's better – no puffs in the playground." His brother and a few other children were giggling with him.

Luckily, Dad didn't seem to hear, but he looked thoughtful as we walked home.

We'd moved into a smaller house since Dad had lost his job. It actually belonged to Uncle Alfie and used to be a farm labourer's cottage. It was only a short distance from school on the outskirts of town and backed onto farmland. We all preferred it to our bigger house, even though we had less space. Somehow it was more cosy and friendly and I loved that my tiny bedroom was in the attic. The staircase to it was behind a cupboard door, so I always felt my bedroom was a secret, magical place.

It had a stunning view across the fields to the woods behind and I liked to stare out of the window, hypnotised by the long green grass changing to silver-blue and then back to green as it bowed in ripples with the wind. Eventually, my gaze would reach the crowd of trees being held back from the field by an old rickety fence. I imagined the trees were all clamouring at the fence, pleading to be allowed into the field for a space to allow them to spread out their branches. How could one grouchy, decrepit, old fence hold all those giants back? If I hanged my head far enough out of the window, I could see the sun rise in the east and set in the west. Some of the pinks and oranges were spectacular, I could certainly understand why people used to worship sun gods.

My day-dreaming would drift to the types of animals that might live in the woods. Dad had given me a book he used to have when he was a child, which showed all the different tracks animals made and the types of food they ate. My imagination would wander through the woods, watching the animals going about their busy little lives. It was when I moved into this room that my literacy marks began to go up at school. My teacher asked me where I got my imagination from and I told her that whenever I looked out of my bedroom window, stories would just drift across the field towards me. She smiled, but I don't think she really understood.

Once we got home from school that day, I went upstairs as usual to get changed. When I came down again Dad was waiting with my delicious hot chocolate. "Are you having problems with Greg Carlton?" I looked up at him in surprise. "I understand he's an intimidating person and I know what his dad is like, but you can't let people dictate to you what you can and can't do with your life."

"It's nothing," I mumbled.

He was quiet for a while, then he sighed. "Okay, I won't push you, but if you want to talk to me anytime, I'm always ready to listen."

Realising that he knew exactly why I'd asked him to stay out of the playground, I focused on my hot drink, unable to admit to my weakness.

Since moving to the cottage, Dad had been in his element teaching me all about the countryside. He had grown up in the country and knew all sorts of interesting things about the wildlife. He could name any species of bird that came to feed from our home-made bird feasts in the little garden, and we would often go searching for animal tracks in the fields and the woods behind. Dad would explain to me how to identify what animal had passed through. It turned out Dad was also a very good tree climber and den builder. Life is full of surprises.

There were some things Dad wasn't good at though. Twice I'd had to go to school in an accidentally pink T-shirt. It was okay for Rosie when her white baby-grows became pink, but I got teased at school and Mum had to buy me a new school T-shirt. Mum laughed when Dad realised one of his own shirts was also pink.

"It's all a learning curve," he assured her as he winked at me and turned back to burning our tea.

Apart from the nasty comments from Grotty Greg and his brother at home-time, I loved having Dad around and I quickly adapted to our new life.

Another advantage of where we now lived, was that I didn't need to go to the park to play out anymore. I never really liked the park because that was where Grotty Greg hung out and even if it wasn't me he was intimidating, I was always on full alert for the next nasty word. The worst thing was, that whenever he picked on me, some of the kids who didn't normally bother me, were so relieved he wasn't picking on *them*, they would join in with him laughing at me. In the countryside, it was quiet and peaceful. The animals never mocked me.

During weekends and holidays, my best friend Ahmed rode over on his mountain bike and played in the fields with me. Ahmed is my only proper friend. If he was at the park when Greg started on me, he would back me up, I know he would, but Greg never started on me when he was around.

Ahmed was smaller and thinner than me, but incredibly strong for his size. Very athletic too, he could run faster than me, jump higher than me and was the best footballer in our school. You would think this would make him big-headed, but it didn't. He was full of fun and adventure and we spent hours creating dens in the woods pretending to be in the army looking out for the enemy, usually a squirrel. Ahmed knew all about the army because his dad was away, Fighting for our Queen and country, he proudly informed me. He talked a lot about his dad, I think it helped him to feel close while he was away and he'd recently got his thick black hair shaved to a 'number two' all over exactly like his dad's. He and his dad looked alike, they both had the same long straight nose flaring to wide nostrils at the end and they both had really dark brown eyes, almost black under jet-black brows. When they were talking to you, they looked totally absorbed in what you were saying. Even if what you were saying wasn't very interesting.

Ahmed listened intently to my plans for a bike course in the woods and helped me make it even better than I imagined with lots of jumps and berms. We would stagger back at the end of the day happily exhausted, hungry enough to guzzle down a bowl of Dad's disgusting home-made broccoli and cheese soup.

One day, as I came out of the playground to meet Dad, Rosie and Sam, Dad looked excited. "Rosie and I have been to the library," Dad whispered as soon as we were out of ear shot from the other children and parents. "We've got a very special book for you. You have to promise me first, that you will tell no-one about this. Not even Ahmed. This has to be kept secret to our family only…" he paused dramatically, "…otherwise there could be terrible consequences."

I raised my eyebrows, but dad wasn't going to say anymore for now. Of course I agreed unreservedly. A secret. A real, proper family secret. This was going to be so exciting. I looked at Rosie and she gave me her lopsided grin. She was keeping the secret too.

CHAPTER 4

* GREG *

Me head was tingling like mad. It was like I was being tasered by a million little pixie police. I was trying to tell meself not to be scared, and then I realised I was holding me breath. I'd have to breathe soon. Slowly, very slowly, I turned me head. The hairs were still standing up on me neck and I'm pretty sure the squirrel's hairs were standing up as well. Eventually, I'd twisted far enough to see the enemy.

A dog. A daft Labrador. Staring at me with his head to one side and his ears pricked up. Probably wondering why I wasn't moving. I couldn't believe it, I'd expected to see a wolf or sommat. He was one of them Golden Labradors with big soft brown eyes and a jet-black nose. He looked dead gentle and friendly-like, but I couldn't be sure. "Where the hell have yer come from?" I growled at him. He wagged his tail and came straight up to me. "Yer should be careful," I warned, "how d'yer know I'm not gunna hurt yer?" I raised me hand as if I was gunna hit him and he licked it and sat on me foot. Just then I heard a whistle and he ran back the way he'd come. I shook me head and went back to looking into the river.

I dunno how long I stayed there, but eventually I realised it was getting dark. I didn't wanna be in the woods on me own in the dark, so even though I didn't wanna go home, I headed back anyway.

There was hell on when I got back. Me dad had taken our dog, Rocky, round the block for a walk to sort his head out. When he'd got home an old bloke had dumped a bag of Rocky's crap on our garden. Angry and drunk, and egged on by all our family, Dad had gone out shouting and swearing at him. When the old bloke stood his ground me dad punched him so hard he fell flat on his back without even putting his arms out. He was out stone cold.

By the time I got there, the ambulance had taken the old bloke away and the coppers were trying to arrest me dad, with the rest of the family trying to stop them. Sommat inside me just exploded and I threw meself at one of the coppers who was trying to handcuff me dad.

The whole street was coming out to watch. I hated them for staring. I hated me relatives for wanting me dad to fight. I hated me mam for screaming. I hated me dad for getting into trouble *again*. I hated the coppers for making things worse. I hated meself. I hated the world. I ran upstairs and punched the bedroom wall so hard me knuckles bled.

I dunno what time I fell asleep. When I went downstairs in the morning me mam was watching cartoons cuddled up with me kid brother. I could see she'd been crying. I didn't wanna know. I went out the front door, slamming it behind me and stomped across to the park.

Anger was boiling inside me. As I sat hunched up with me back against the cold wind, I thought about the night before. The scrap, the sirens, the nosy neighbours. Dad was supposed to be taking me to the match today but the police hadn't let him come home yet. Another promise broken. Another birthday messed up by his antics. No doubt it would become another one of me dad's hugely hilarious stories when he retold it over the years, but right now all I knew was that me dad had been arrested, me birthday had been ruined and me family was the talk of the street. *Again*. Who'd come out to watch and laugh at us last night?

Looking up, I saw a woman walking towards me with her kid. She looked at me and then looked down. *Was she trying to hide a laugh? Was she laughing at me?* She turned away to push her kid on the swing, or hide her laughter. I looked back down at the bench I was sitting on to avoid looking at her anymore. Finding a stiff twig, I began to carve me initials into the bench, then I crisscrossed over them. An old hag walked by dragging her shopping trolley. I wasn't stupid. I knew she walked past me on purpose to have a look at the kid from *that* family. She looked directly at me and tutted.

"Who the hell are yer tutting at?" I snarled. She flinched and carried on her way.

I dragged the stick backwards and forwards across me name. Filled with hate and hating me life.

The wind was picking up and making me cold, but I stayed at the park and tried not to shiver. A boy came skipping into the park. He looked so irritatingly happy and pleased with himself. He was rubbing his happiness in me face. I felt me fists clench, I really, really wanted to punch that stupid smile off his face, but his dad was with him so I just glared at him as they passed. I started to feel trapped at the park. More and more people kept coming and it seemed like they were winding me up on purpose. I didn't wanna go back to the miserable pit that is our home. No doubt me friends would be getting ready to go to the match with their dads, but me dad was still in the nick, so where did that leave me? Where could *I* go? Then I remembered. I took off in the same direction I'd gone yesterday.

Eventually, I reached the woods and found me little bridge. It was just as peaceful as before. As if last night had never happened. That was just a nightmare. But I knew last night was real so this must be the dream.

It wasn't as cold here, the trees were sheltering me from the bitter wind. Like yesterday, I watched the leaves float under the bridge and disappear around the bend. Like yesterday, I slowly felt me heart beat begin to calm and me fists unclench. I hadn't even realised that they were still clenched 'til I felt them begin to uncurl. Me head was throbbing and I rubbed me temples. I focused on the colours surrounding me. They didn't seem as bright as yesterday, maybe 'cos they weren't wet. The dullness made them look softer, made the woods seem even more friendly. I wondered about following the track further into the woods but wasn't sure what I would find there or if I could find me way back.

The calmness soothed me head, but after a while I began to get that strange tickly sensation like last time I was here. Gradually, the bubbles I'd seen before started to reappear in front of me eyes. As I watched them, they began to come together and I started to remember about the dog that had come. I looked up and there he was trotting towards me.

The daft dog came straight up as if we'd always been best friends, gave me a lick, and carried on his way. Just as he was about to be out of sight he stopped and looked back at me with his head cocked to one side and his ears pricked up. I felt like he was signalling me to follow, like the dogs on those silly kids' programmes.

He'd made me mind up for me, I followed him along the path. I got the feeling he was on the trail of sommat the way his tail was wagging so fast from side to side and he never lifted his nose off the ground. We were walking like that for ages, until half way up a bank he stopped and stared at a fairly big hole. A fox hole probably. He pricked his ears forward and began to pant. Then he looked back at me.

"D'yer want me to take a look?" I asked him and then laughed at meself for talking to a dog. He looked back at the hole and made a grumbling sound, still wagging his tail. "Okay ya daft dog." I agreed and looked in.

I couldn't see much, but obviously sommat lived there. There was some old hay and grass and leaves that looked like they'd been dragged out of the hole and some big paw prints with claws in that looked a lot longer than the Labrador's. "I'm not putting me hand in there," I told him. "The fox might come out and bite me."

Nearby, I noticed a tree stump with deep scratch marks on it. The fox must've attacked the tree, I guessed, probably mistaking it for a human. I definitely wasn't putting me hand in the hole.

There was more daylight here and I realised we'd almost come out the other side of the woods. There was an old broken fence at the edge, a field and then a small cottage. The dog turned away and padded back towards the bridge, so I followed him back into the safety of the woods.

This was the beginning of the first proper friendship I ever had. I had friends and cousins who I hung out with, but I was the hard one in the group. The others looked up to me and admired me for me fighting skills and the fear others had of me. I knew they hung around with me 'cos it made them look hard. It had become second nature to me to always be looking for a fight – to play the part expected of me.

The Labrador didn't need me to be anyone. He just liked to sit on me feet and look up at me with a real soft look in his eye. I felt like he knew everything I was thinking and I understood him too. It was like we were talking without needing to actually open our mouths and make any sounds. When I was feeling sad, he knew and he leaned against me and licked me face. When I was happy he'd get all playful and fetch me sticks to throw for him or roll over for his belly to be tickled. If anyone had seen me with him, I would never, *ever* have lived it down.

Over the weeks and months, I took to sneaking little bits of food out of the house especially for him. He always seemed to know when I was coming and would be there waiting for me. I didn't know if he had a home or if he'd got lost and made the woods his home.

I reckoned I should give him a name. First of all I thought of Rocky, the name of our latest dog. But I'd never really got close with Rocky. He lived in an outdoor kennel in the garden and our mam wouldn't let me and me kid brother go out and pet him unless our dad was with us 'cos he could be vicious. He'd never harmed me. In fact, he was always calm when I went near him, but he'd gone for me brother when he'd thrown stones at him. Me dad had gone out with a metal pole and beaten the dog so hard he'd expected it to be dead the next morning. It survived and me dad said it would never go near a kid again, but me mam wouldn't listen. It was the only time she's got her own way with our dad, and we were never allowed near Rocky again.

I decided to call the Labrador Andrew. Andrew is me middle name. It made me feel as if we had a connection and I liked that. "You're more like family than anyone I'm actually related to," I whispered to him. He wagged his tail. I swear he understood exactly what I meant.

The only weird thing was the tickling sensation on me skin and the gentle tingling in me head and the fuzzy bubbles I kept seeing in front of me eyes. It didn't bother me, I kind of liked it and it didn't happen very often. It never happened outside the woods and I was sure it was only when Andrew or another animal was near. But that doesn't make no sense. Does it?

CHAPTER 5

* JAMES *

The walk back home seemed to take forever. Dad refused to say anything more about the secret in case anyone overheard.

Finally, we reached home. The book was neatly placed in the centre of the coffee table. It was a nature tracking book and inside was a bookmark. I turned to the page indicated which showed an animal hole in some woodland. It was labelled 'Badger Sett'.

My dad grinned. "I was walking Sam this morning and he got very excited. Far more excited than when he sees a squirrel," Dad explained. "He started tracking. I could barely keep up with poor Rosie bouncing in the back-carrier but when we got across the bridge in the woods I saw a clue to what he was tracking: those prints there in the book. I saw them in the mud at the side of the stream. I looked around the edge of the woods, and just inside the woods, not far from the field..." He dropped his voice, "I found a badger sett. Exactly like that one in the book."

I gasped. Dad always spoke about badgers in a revered whisper. They were the 'enigmatic creatures of the night' as he liked to refer to them. Despite growing up in the countryside, Dad had never been lucky enough to see a real-life badger – apart from road kill – but he'd never given up hope.

Dad looked at me with a serious expression on his face. "If I tell you where the sett is," he began in a stern whisper, "you *have* to swear to secrecy. Badgers are protected, and interfering with a sett is a criminal offence. Some evil people, excited by their aggressive reputation, would risk prison to set dogs on them to fight to the death. The poor badgers don't even deserve their aggressive reputation, they only fight in self-defence to protect their young or their territory. We cannot be the cause of these beautiful animals being set upon."

"I'll keep the secret, Dad. I swear." I made a cross over my heart with my finger.

He nodded. "I know you will, son. We both will, because if the wrong people find out about the sett, we'll be condemning the badgers to a terrible, terrifying death.

"I'll show you where the sett is, and on the way we need to keep an eye out for any other clues that indicate we might have badgers nearby.

"I'm ninety percent sure it is a badger sett, but I can't completely rule out that it is a fox den, or that foxes are using an old discarded badger sett. The footprint I found was a bit smudged. I'm worried I could have made a mistake, so we need to find more clues."

"What about left-over food, Dad? Will we be able to tell by what food they leave near their sett?"

Dad stopped what he was doing and looked at me thoughtfully, then he smiled. "Well son, they eat their food wherever they find it, but you've given me an idea. Although badgers are omnivores, so they'll eat pretty much anything, their favourite food is worms and they eat hundreds of them, leaving little snuffle holes in the ground where they've been hunting for them. Let's keep an eye out for snuffle holes in the field.

"Now hurry upstairs and get changed, we'll have a look before tea."

I ran upstairs and grabbed my magnifying glass. I felt just like Sherlock Holmes hunting for clues. Dad put Rosie in the back-carrier and as we walked across the field together, I couldn't help feeling proud. I didn't care what the bullies at school said anymore. My dad was the best. He knew more than most people about animals and nature and building dens. I loved spending time with him.

When we got closer to the woods, we started to notice the ground had been disturbed in places. It could have been a badger, but it could have been rabbits. It was hard to tell. We walked backwards and forwards examining the holes and I used my magnifying glass to see if I could make out a smaller hole within the hole where a worm might have been sucked out of the ground the way we suck up spaghetti, but I couldn't find anything obvious.

After a while, Rosie started crying. I don't think she found badger tracking as exciting as Dad and me. Then Dad remembered he should be cooking dinner and Mum was due home from work, so we hurried back to tell her all about what we'd found.

Mum was just as excited as us about our discovery and started looking through the book that Dad had borrowed from the library.

"Oh look here," said Mum, "badgers live better than us. They don't just have one home, they have a few smaller holiday homes too. And they're ever so clean, they change their bedding every couple of days and they toilet outside instead of fouling their sett."

"Well I know I don't manage to wash our bedding as often as you'd like, but we all do our business in a toilet and not in our bedroom or the living room, so we're doing as well as the badgers there," teased Dad. "And anyway, if you're jealous of the way badgers live, just think, instead of the lovely dinner I'm cooking you tonight, you'd be eating hundreds of worms instead."

Mum paused just a little too long, before replying, "Yes love, *of course* your meals are better than worms." We both chuckled.

From the book, we discovered that badgers can even eat hedgehogs. Sam presses hedgehogs with his nose then yelps because they've curled up and the spines have pricked him, but a badger can cleverly uncurl a hedgehog and chew through its unprotected belly to eat it. Gross!

Every day after school, I would go over to the sett with Dad, just to stand there and look. It took a while for me to notice, but once we got used to seeing it all the time, we started to notice a path that led up to it. Generations of badgers must have used the same path to reach the sett, and over the years, the earth had worn slightly lower than the surroundings. You could only see it once you knew it was there though. A bit like when you write a secret message to your friend in lemon juice. If they don't know it's there, they won't know to heat it with an iron to read it. I loved that we had discovered a secret badger path.

It was frustrating that badgers come out at night instead of the day, this rendered my dad's old binoculars useless, although it didn't stop me from peering across the field in the middle of the night hoping for a glimpse – perhaps a pair of glowing eyes in the dark. I wished we could afford a pair of night vision binoculars.

Sometimes we walked down to the river where dad had first seen the print, hoping to find another one. If it had five toes rather than four we would know it was a badger rather than a fox or a dog. The problem was the animals we were tracking seemed to put their back feet where their front feet had just been so any prints we found were smudged. We forced some brambles closer together either side of the path near the sett to see if we could catch some hair and discover whether the animal using it was black and white or red.

One morning, I woke up and noticed that the walls of my room had a strange blueish glow. I opened the curtains and saw the most glorious sight – everywhere was covered in thick, glittery snow. I pulled my wellies on, threw my coat over my pyjamas, and ran outside. By the time Mum and Dad and Rosie had got up, I'd already made a snowman. I thought the day couldn't get better, then my dad called me in, told me to get dressed and said we were going tracking.

As soon as we entered the field, we saw lots of rabbit prints zigzagging all over the place. There were bird prints too, starting from nowhere and disappearing where they had taken flight again.

We were halfway across the field when we thought we could make out some kind of long dent in the snow. As we reached it, we could see that it was a path that had been made by animals. It looked like it led to and from the badger sett. Quietly and carefully, we followed the trail. Most of the prints were smudged, but here and there we could see a clear print: five toes with long claws. There was no mistake now, we were definitely tracking a badger clan rather than a skulk of foxes.

Dad was just as excited as me when we ran back to tell Mum what we'd found. She suggested I keep a diary about the badger family, so from that day forward I noted the date of each clue they left for us. I also made a note of any other animal tracks we found near or around the sett. There were always plenty of bird, squirrel and rabbit prints. There were also human footprints, which must have been ours, so I didn't record those ones. Sometimes we thought we found fox prints but weren't absolutely sure they were not Sam's prints as he treated the field and the woods as an extension of our garden. Sam could easily push through the garden hedge and wandered at will in the woods, leaving a trail of footprints. He would always come charging back to us when he heard our whistle.

That was another thing Dad taught me – how to whistle with my fingers in my mouth, which creates a very high-pitched shrill sound. I became a bit of a playground celebrity with that skill. My whistle was so loud and clear Ahmed reckoned I could be heard over a mile away.

CHAPTER 6

* GREG *

When Dad got nicked after the dog crap incident, he'd nearly been sent down. He was let out on bail, but he had to behave himself or he'd be back inside. It'd been quiet without him for twenty-four hours, but the minute he got home everything went back to normal. In fact, from that day on, the atmosphere in the house got worse and worse. Mam cried all the time these days without even trying to hide it, and they were both drinking and getting into arguments and fights every day. I'd lie awake at night listening to them, and I hated them both for being like that.

One night, me mam was threatening to call the cops on me dad. He was screaming he'd rather do himself in than be sent back down. Me kid brother crept into me room, I could tell he was proper scared 'cos his eyes were massive and he was shaking. He knew he wasn't allowed in me room and was risking a hiding from me, but he was even more scared of all the banging and crashing and screaming he could hear downstairs. He was trying hard not to cry 'cos I hate crying, but his breathing was all jerky. For the first time, I actually felt a teeny bit sorry for him, so I let him climb into bed with me. He wrapped his arms round me so tight I could hardly breathe and he fell asleep whimpering into me chest. I couldn't remember the last time anyone had hugged me, but nobody could see and in the morning I'd make sure he didn't tell anyone.

I looked down at him sleeping curled up against me. I'd always hated his floppy blond hair – it made him look weak. And his long soft lashes framing his baby blue eyes – he should've been a girl. They looked even darker and longer with wet tears dripping off them. He didn't suit a name as strong as Kyle – Kylie would have suited him better. Poor kid. As I looked at him, I stopped feeling jealous of his special bond with Mam. These days, Mam didn't spend much time with him anyway. She was too busy feeling sorry for herself. I'd rather never've had me mam's love than be favourite then rejected like he was. His dad despised him, his mother didn't care. If I was his best bet for attention , he was not doing well at all. I let him stay all night.

In the morning, I dug me finger into his side to wake him and he scampered back to his own room without saying a word.

I crept out of the house and reached school early. I hated school but I'd rather be at school than be around when me dad gets up and starts yelling at me mam for there being no food in the place. Then she comes down looking half dead and hungover and having a go back at him. Anyhow, Mrs Appleton always lets me have some toast when I turn up early.

I was sneaking out of the house unnoticed more and more. Either going to school or bunking off to the woods. No-one asked me where I was going or where I'd been. No-one cared. If anyone *had* asked, I would've given them a right mouthful. Even the teachers were wary of me. I was failing badly at school but no-one dared to question me. I still had me reputation.

At the woods, I knew Andrew would be waiting for me and he'd be excited to see me. I always knew when he was near 'cos I'd get them funny sensations again. He usually waited for me on our bridge wagging his tail. It was like his tail was a magic brush sweeping away everything bad in me life. On the bridge, it was just me and him.

Over the months we'd become best friends – was I a nutter to think of him as me best friend? He knew all me secrets. I think he tried to share his with me too. He often showed me the fox hole he'd found but I still didn't really understand why he wanted me to know about it – other than it was a secret he could share. We would often wander deeper and deeper into the woods together. Whichever way I wanted to go, Andrew knew and would turn that way. He could read me mind. I was never scared of getting lost when I was with Andrew 'cos he knew when I wanted to go back and he'd just turn around and lead the way back to our bridge. Then he'd lick me hand to say bye and trot off to wherever it was he went at night.

I wished I could live in the woods. Just me and Andrew.

* JAMES *

At first I didn't tell Ahmed about our family secret, (or our secret family, depending on how you looked at it). For a little while, I stopped inviting him over because I was worried he would find out, but Dad said that looked suspicious and it was like a test to strengthen my mind, to have my best friend over and still not tell him. Eventually, I invited him over. And I told him straight away. The secret just burst out of me, but I did swear him to secrecy first, and in return, Ahmed told me his secret: that his mum was really a secret spy. I suspected this might not be true, but I didn't question him because Ahmed looked so earnestly at me I didn't want to disappoint him.

It turned out that having a mum as a secret spy was very beneficial, as Ahmed was able to give me lots of tips about spying on the badgers. For starters, he said we must stop going right up to the sett and looking for clues as we were leaving our scent and making the badgers wary. They have their own scents that they recognise each other by and our scent would represent the enemy. I'm not sure how Ahmed's mum knew that, unless she spied on badgers, but we checked in the books and it seemed she was right. We also learned that the clan scent would quickly fade if a badger was away from the sett too long, which causes problems for rescuers as they have less than twenty-four hours to return a rescued badger or it will risk being bullied or even killed by its own family who would mistake it for an enemy. Imagine being attacked by your own family.

It was spring half-term holiday and Dad said he had a project for us. He took us to Uncle Alfie's farm and drove up to the side of the big barn where Uncle Alfie stacks all his rubbish that might one day be useful, such as old tyres, broken fence posts, and the like.

"Your Uncle Alfie said we can have anything we want from this pile." Dad grinned excitedly.

"Erm … okay. Why?"

"You'll soon see. Come on, help me get all this wood stacked onto the trailer."

We found pieces of fencing, some broken pallets and half a shed. We threw it all onto the trailer and Ahmed and I sat on top as we bounced across the fields back to our house. Dad told us to unload it into the garden. He was clearly excited. "We're going to build a tree house," he declared, "and not just any tree house, not only the best tree house in Inglehow – it's also going to be a nature watch hut so we can spy on the badgers."

Ahmed and I looked at each other. We were always building little dens in the woods, but this was going to be the best den ever. At the bottom of our cottage garden, very close to the hedge is an old oak tree with a strong, thick trunk and long branches reaching across the garden. We looked at the tree, looked back at each other, and grinned. Perfect!

We soon became skilled at using Dad's crowbar to prise the planks of wood off the pallets and the old piece of shed. Dad had us pile them up in size order and we had to pull out any nails we found using his claw hammer. By the time we'd finished it was tea time and we were starving. We were also filthy with all the dust sticking to our sweat. Mum was so impressed with how hard we'd worked, she ordered pizzas as a special treat and phoned Ahmed's Mum to let her know he was staying over.

The next morning, I opened my curtains and couldn't believe the huge pile of wood we'd made at the foot of the oak tree. I hadn't realised how big it had got as we were doing it, but seeing it the next day on fresh eyes, I could see just how much work we had done.

I woke Ahmed up and we got dressed as quickly as we could and bounded down the stairs to go out to the garden.

"Where do you two think you are going?" asked Dad.

"Oh, Dad, can't we just skip breakfast today?" I moaned.

No chance. Dad always said breakfast was the most important meal of the day. He made us his special breakfast he calls 'Pink Stuff,' which is eggs, tinned tomatoes and cheese all beaten together fried and slopped onto toast. It tastes nearly as bad as it looks. Ahmed once politely declared that he loved it, and as karma for lying, Dad believed him and has made it for us every weekend that Ahmed has stayed over ever since.

"Right, now you're battle ready," laughed Dad. We all marched to the bottom of the garden. Dad climbed up the branches into the centre of the tree and instructed us to pass him the fence posts. They were so heavy, Ahmed and I had to work together to hand each one up to Dad, who positioned them in the branches and attached them with binder twine, creating a strong frame.

Next, we had to hand up the largest planks of wood so Dad could make a sturdy floor. It took ages, because he had to keep sawing round where the branches protruded, but eventually the floor was finished and Ahmed and I could come up and stand on it. It gave a great view over the hedge, across the field and into the woods. We could just make out the arched entrance to the badger sett.

Now we needed to build the walls. We passed up more planks which Dad put roughly in position, then he let Ahmed and I take turns hammering them onto the frame. It was hot work so Mum kept popping down the garden with lemonade. The branches caused us some problems the way they bent this way and that way between the planks, but they were also making the whole den unique and magical, with little hidey holes for our snacks and equipment. Dad taught Ahmed and me how to use a saw and we cut a long thin slot in the direction of the sett. It was wide enough for all three of us to look through at the same time but not very high so our den wouldn't get too much wind in and, as Ahmed reminded us, to make sure the badgers wouldn't pick up our scent.

Ahmed and I thought we'd never get to sleep that night with the excitement of seeing our den developing, but I think we were asleep before our heads even hit the pillows.

We couldn't believe it the next morning when we realised we'd slept in late. It was nearly midday when we woke up, but at least we missed out on Pink Stuff and skipped straight to lunch. Dad had made pea and ham soup – it was no better than his cheese and broccoli soup, but we gulped it down, desperate to get back outside to finish the den.

Our last job was to construct the roof. We crisscrossed some garden canes and thin pieces of wood from the frame to the branches higher up, then nailed on some old plastic feed-sacks to make it waterproof. We jumped down and looked at it. The brightly coloured plastic sacks looked awful and stood out a mile.

"Don't worry," Ahmed beamed, "I saw some old chicken wire at the farm, let's collect it and stretch it across the roof, then we can weave fallen branches from the woods into it, like my dad does with cargo nets to camouflage army equipment. You'll never know it was there."

By the time we were finished, we were exhausted, covered in scratches and dirt, and absolutely starving. We stepped back and admired our work. If you blurred your eyes, it wasn't really obvious that there was a den there at all. Mum and Rosie came down the garden to see the result of our hard work.

"This is amazing," Mum laughed. "Rosie will love it too when she's old enough to climb up."

The next day, Ahmed and I sneaked downstairs early without waking Dad. We couldn't wait to play in our den. Ahmed climbed up first. "You'll never guess what's in here."

I hurried up behind him. Strung up around the top of the walls were some old battery powered fairy lights. There were some cushions on the floor and our pile of badger books were on a branch that was acting as a shelf. In one of the nooks we found Dad's old binoculars and in another we found a torch. A third hidey hole held a biscuit tin, which we quickly discovered was crammed full of chocolate chip cookies. Today was going to be the best day ever.

We could never get a good mobile signal out here in the countryside, especially in the woods, so I came up with the great idea of using Rosie's old baby monitor so we could communicate with each other when one of us was in the den and the other was somewhere else in the woods, although the range didn't go very far.

It was so much fun playing army games all day that we were disappointed to have to go back to my bedroom to sleep. We really wanted to sleep in the den. In fact, we wanted to sleep, eat, and live in the den, but Dad said the nights were still too cold. He promised that as soon as the weather got milder, he would let Ahmed and me sleep in the den overnight to spy on the clan. The summer seemed so far away. We couldn't wait.

CHAPTER 7

* GREG *

One evening, I'd only just got back home from the woods when the shouting started again. I couldn't bear it. Me and Andrew had had a peaceful afternoon in the woods and then me mood was always spoiled as soon as I got back home again.

Unlike Andrew, me Mam and Dad never seemed pleased to see me – if they even noticed me. All they cared about was where their next drink was coming from and whose fault anything and everything was. They accused each other of drinking too much, of not doing any work, of this and that. They should've looked in a mirror – they were both just as bad as each other.

I looked at them both. Neither of them had heard me come in. Me Mam's hair was all over her red blotchy face like it had been blown there but there was no wind in the living room. There was a cup of tea spilled onto the carpet and a broken plate with biscuits scattered about. Once over, me mam would've leaped up to clean it and the living room would've been back to spotless in seconds. But not now. I don't think me mam ever cleaned up nomore. The ashtrays were always overflowing with fag ends. Beer cans and empty crisp packets covered the floor. The curtains that used to be neatly fastened back in big swags were bunched up and trapped by the back of the sofa. I couldn't remember the last time I brought a friend home. I was too embarrassed.

Flinging me coat back on, I grabbed a torch and went straight back out. Nobody asked me where I was going. Nobody noticed me go. Nobody cared whether I was there or not.

It was February half-term but the weather was weirdly warm. I ran straight back to the woods. I don't know what I'd planned, but the woods had become me sanctuary. Me bolt hole. I expected Andrew to be there on the bridge waiting for me, but he wasn't. I walked up to his beloved hole but he wasn't there neither. Suddenly, I felt really, really lonely. I scraped some leaves together against the broad trunk of a tree and settled down for the night.

The nighttime was a lot colder and more uncomfortable than I'd imagined, and I didn't manage to grab a wink of sleep. There were loads of strange noises in the woods. Every now and then, I heard a strange unearthly scream that I told meself was a wild animal but definitely sounded like something undead. I forced meself to stay all night but decided to bring a blade next time for protection.

As the sun came up, me stomach rumbled and I

realised I hadn't had no tea – now it was only a few hours to breakfast time. I guessed it was about five in the morning. Me legs had become so stiff I had to use the tree trunk to support me as I stood up. I began to wander home, wondering what I would tell me family about where I'd been.

I didn't wanna tell them about the woods – that was me secret sanctuary, but they'd've been out of their minds with worry. Probably the police had been called, and me family hated the police. What excuse could I make up? I couldn't pretend I'd been at a friend's 'cos they'd have already phoned them all. I was gunna be in big trouble. But then again, maybe after all the worry they'd be pleased to see me and realise it was their fault. Maybe we could go back to being a normal family again.

I pictured me mam giving me a big hug – probably crying again. And me dad giving me a playful punch and making some joke about all the people out looking for me and what a tearaway I was. I even pictured me kid brother giving me another hug. I decided I'd let him hug me a few sneaky seconds before pushing him away – I had to keep me reputation. For the first time in ages I was looking forward to going home even though I knew I'd be in loads of trouble.

As I walked up our street it was spookily quiet. The woods had been quiet as well, but that was a different kind of quiet. I'd never known our street to be so quiet before. Not that I'd walked along it at five in the morning before.

I tiptoed up to our house.
Silence.

I tried the front door.

Locked.

I tried very hard to walk quietly round the back without disturbing Rocky. The stupid dog began to bark.

"Shh it's me," I whispered at him. He looked straight at me, cocked his head on one side and stopped barking. Phew!

The back door was unlocked. I crept upstairs and into bed. Nobody had noticed me come home. Nobody had noticed I was missing. At least I didn't need to lie and make excuses. But I felt empty inside. Nobody cared. I wasn't being dramatic or nowt. Nobody actually cared. Suddenly, I wasn't hungry anymore. I laid there staring at the ceiling. Feeling empty.

* JAMES *

It was going to be our first night in the den, we were unbelievably excited. "Crikey, Mum's given us enough stuff to last all summer." I laughed as Ahmed and I heaved the heavy bags down the garden.

Dad, Ahmed and I were supposed to be taking turns keeping watch while two of us slept, but in reality, all three of us were too excited to fall asleep. Lying on our tummies in the khaki coloured sleeping bags, it was hard to see anything at first. The moon was casting a little light, but not on the badger sett where the canopy of trees was blocking it. I stared and stared until gradually I was able to make out various shades of shapes in shadows. I could just make out the old rickety fence and the trees behind. Dad noticed the sounds first. We'd left Rosie's baby monitor as close to the sett as we had dared, and now we could hear scuffling sounds coming from it. We stared with anticipation at the dark hole in the woods.

As we peered down into the blackness below, a bulky shape appeared. We strained and strained our eyes but we really couldn't make out what animal we were watching. I knew if I switched my torch on, it would frighten the animal away, but if I didn't, I would never know for definite what we were looking at. *Should I take the risk and switch it on?* I strained my eyes but I still couldn't see. Finally, in frustration I switched on my torch and we glimpsed a flash of black and white fur as it dashed back into its hole. We hadn't seen much, but it was our first ever glimpse of a real, live badger. We waited in vain for a reappearance, but eventually about five o'clock, cold and exhausted, we trudged back up the garden and went to bed dreaming of badgers.

The next weekend when Ahmed came, he could hardly contain his excitement. His dad had come home and he had brought army issue infrared binoculars with him. Dad raised his eyebrows at mum and she quickly shook her head. They weren't going to ask any awkward questions about how he'd managed to persuade the army to allow him to take home restricted expensive equipment.

We set up camp in the den again and watched with eager expectation. This time as the badgers crept out there would be no bright light to frighten them back inside. We took turns with the night vision binoculars, but nothing moved. I fretted that my torch had scared them away from their home and they'd had to move into one of their other setts out of sight. I watched for as long as my eyes would let me but I was beginning to lose focus, so reluctantly I passed the binoculars to Ahmed. A little while later Ahmed passed the binoculars to Dad. Still nothing. My stomach started to knot with disappointment. If only I'd had more patience last week. Dad passed the binoculars back to me.

What was that? Was it my imagination or was there some movement? I shushed Ahmed and Dad even though they weren't making any noise and peered harder through the binoculars. Very slowly, a large shape emerged from the sett. It snuffled around a bit then began to reverse back in. I held my breath. It came forward again and this time it was accompanied by another shape almost as big. I knew I should let Ahmed watch – these were his binoculars after all, but I couldn't tear myself away as a third shape came out. Then two smaller but similarly shaped animals followed. Babies? They snuffled around not far from the entrance to the sett, seemingly suspicious. Dad prised the binoculars from my hands and handed them to Ahmed. Amazingly the badgers stayed long enough for Dad to watch them too.

"Let's give them all names," I suggested.

We called the boar Mr Blake after dad's *boring* geography teacher from school who he always joked about. We named the sows Mrs Blake and Aunty Blake, although we couldn't actually tell the difference between them so we were never quite sure which one we were talking about. The two cubs we named Brock and Belinda. Again, we weren't sure if they were a boy and a girl, but one was slightly smaller than the other so we guessed it was a girl. Dad estimated the cubs were only about five or six months old as they're usually born around February.

Once the whole family was out of the sett, Mr Blake seemed to relax a little, and started foraging for food while making gentle grunting noises. They ventured further into the field away from the trees and into the moonlight. Belinda and Brock were like a pair of circus clowns, bounding around Mr Blake. Brock kept trying to jump over Mr Blake but he could only jump about half way up then would fall onto his back. Belinda somehow always got in the way and he would land on top of her causing her to shriek at him, then she'd chase him round and round Mr Blake, totally getting in the way of his foraging but he didn't seem to mind. Now and again, he'd join in and bat them over their heads with his front paw in what looked like an animal attempt at a head lock. If they got too boisterous he'd nip at their ears, but it was obvious he was just gently telling them off – we'd read that badgers have hugely powerful jaws and can lock them together so that whatever they have bitten cannot escape.

Aunty Blake didn't seem as tolerant of the cubs. She played with them for a little while, but then she shook them off and nipped at them. Mrs Blake, however, seemed to enjoy the attention and let them climb across her and fool around. She kept rolling over and play wrestling them and they all made lovely chittering noises that sounded so friendly. The sound was like nothing I'd heard before – somewhere between a cat purring and a pig grunting with a bit of chicken clucking thrown in for good measure.

Over the summer months, we settled into a routine of watching the badgers come out to play before they crept off across the fields or into the depths of the woods to hunt for food. Brock and Belinda were relentless in their play. Mr and Mrs Blake would play with them for ages before going to 'work' to look for grubs to eat. The cubs favourite game seemed to be 'King of the Castle' on a tree stump next to their sett, and we realised that was why it was covered in scratches, but they were just as likely to use poor old Mrs Blake as the castle. They kept falling off though, because Mrs Blake would continue to forage for food with them sitting on her back, although this never stopped them from trying. Again and again and again.

The high-spirited cubs also seemed to be fond of playing tag. Brock would start by chasing Belinda round the sett and the tree stump, then when he caught her she would spin round and chase him back. It was so funny to see them playing the same games we played at school. The cubs frequently crashed into Aunty Blake, causing her to shriek at them. We couldn't work out if this was accidental bumping due to poor eyesight or if they were being naughty and bumping into her on purpose. Often, the whole family would relax together spending ages grooming each other. Dad said they were picking fleas off each other and they certainly did scratch a lot.

Eventually, when the badgers disappeared from view into the darkness of the woods, we'd snuggle down into our sleeping bags and fall asleep. We loved sleeping in the den and wished we could move in permanently. I continued to fill in my diary and I added detailed drawings of them playing and foraging. We never tired of our covert operation, in fact it remained just as exciting every time we went to our look-out, but nothing prepared us for what was to come.

CHAPTER 8

* GREG *

During weekends I'd started staying over at me Uncle Kev's. His hobby was messing about with cars and he let me help him restore his old Mini. He'd been working on the Mini all me life and it didn't look any closer to being finished, but Aunty Anne said if he was "fiddling in the garage it kept him out of trouble". I wondered if she sometimes sneaked into the garage and interfered with the restoration just to keep him in there longer.

It was Sunday evening and Uncle Kev was insisting I go back home 'cos I had school the next day. He seemed to understand how much I hated home but sometimes he would become indifferent and say I lived there with me parents not here with him.

I threw down the wheel brace I'd been using and stormed back towards our street. I had to pass the park on the way and saw that the Summer Fair must be coming to town 'cos the gypsy horses were tied to the trees. A crowd of kids from the estate had gathered round daring each other to touch one of the horses. "Greg'll climb on one. He's not scared," one of them shouted. He was right – I wasn't scared. But I wasn't his puppet neither. I walked on, ignoring them.

"Hello love." Me mam greeted me as though I'd just been out for a stroll – not missing since Friday morning. For all she knew or cared I mightn't've been at Uncle Kev's. I might've been laid dead in a ditch. I ignored her and went up the stairs. Kyle looked at me, not knowing whether to speak or not. I shoved him out the way and slammed me door shut.

Me room was exactly as I'd left it. Mouldy dinner plates, bed unmade, dirty clothes on the floor. If me mam had really missed me, surely she'd've made an effort to make me bedroom look half decent? She didn't care. I looked for me favourite CD but couldn't find it. I put another one on instead and let the music block out the world.

A couple of hours passed until me dad came home and I heard the usual rowing begin again. Thanks Dad. Thanks for rushing up to see me. For telling me you'd missed me. Had he even noticed I'd been gone?

I grabbed me coat and went back out to the park to see the horses. It had started raining and the kids had all gone, but now Kyle was there on his own, looking at one of the horses. He was up to sommat. I ducked down behind a hedge to spy on him.

* JAMES *

I was so excited. The fair was in and to finish a great weekend, Ahmed was coming to the fair with us. All day I'd kept imagining the taste of sticky candy floss and the smell of diesel fumes mixed with burgers. If we listened carefully, we could actually hear the sounds of thrilled screams and banging tunes drifting across the fields towards us.

We weren't going until after tea, but Mum and Dad let us walk over to see the fair horses at the park for half an hour before it was time to go.

It was quiet at the park, everyone was either at the fair or the drizzling rain must have been keeping them indoors. As we got closer, we both recognised Greg Carlton's younger brother close to the horses. *What is he doing?* Without needing to communicate with each other we both instinctively crouched behind the large laurel bush and peeked through the leaves. Kyle seemed to be trying to intimidate one of the horses. He kept threatening to hit it, and it would throw up its head then he would shout at it. We kept watching, unsure what to do. We wanted to protect the horse, but no-one got involved with the Carltons if they could help it. Suddenly, Kyle swung his leg round. I thought he was going to kick the horse, but no… he leaped onto its back.

The horse had had enough. It kicked up its hind legs so high it almost did a hand stand and Kyle went flying through the air, wind-milling his arms and legs as he flew. His ear-splitting scream was immediately muffled as he face planted into a steaming fresh pile of horse manure. Staggering to his feet, all I saw was the bright blonde hair on his head contrasting with the dark greeny-brown horse muck all over his face – he looked like a really disgusting ice-cream cornet.

Kyle was gagging and choking and coughed poo up out of his throat. This was too much. This was too funny. Ahmed and I staggered out of the bush squealing with laughter, holding our stomachs and pointing. Kyle was panicking trying to pick the poo out of his nose but he was only succeeding in shoving it further up.

"Help me!" he gargled. By this time my legs seemed to be laughing harder than me. They wobbled and wobbled finally depositing me on the floor. Kyle was rushing towards me "Help me!" he demanded.

"Squash your other nostril closed and snort out," I managed to gasp between peals of laughter. He did, and a perfectly cylindrical poo compound fired out of his nose onto his T-shirt. This was way too much. Now I couldn't breathe, strange chirruping noises were coming from my throat and tears were streaming down my face. Through my tears, another shape emerged. It seemed to be coming towards me at high speed. Gradually, I was able to make out the shape. It was Greg Carlton, charging towards me from the other end of the park. I needed to get a grip, my legs wouldn't work and Greg was getting closer. Ahmed was shouting me. I needed to get up and run. I couldn't. Greg grabbed both my shoulders and head-butted me square on my nose. I stopped laughing.

* GREG *

As if Kyle being thrown from the stupid horse wasn't enough. As if him landing in horse crap wasn't enough. Two daft kids from the primary school had to see it. I gave them a clear message they wouldn't forget in a hurry, and knew they wouldn't dare tell anyone else or they would get what was coming to them, but that didn't make me feel any better.

I dragged Kyle home and shoved him into the shower.

That evening, as I was lying on me bed, I pictured the two kids' smarmy little faces. I remembered them laughing. Laughing at me kid brother. Nobody laughs at me family and gets away with it. I recognised one of them. It was the one with the weird looking dad. I lay rigid on me bed, with me fists curled and a knot in me belly. Staring at me bedroom ceiling, I could hear Mam and Dad still arguing downstairs.

I ran off to the woods. The one place I knew would calm me. I needed to calm down. It had been a rubbish day and I felt real miserable.

Lately, sleeping had become a big problem for me. I hated trying to get to sleep 'cos I'd think about how things used to be at home and how they were now and I'd get more and more angry. Soon, I'd be too angry to sleep and nights without sleep are really, really, long and boring and frustrating.

On the worst nights, I couldn't lie still in me bed and I'd sneak out to the woods. I'd found a better tree, deeper in the woods, that had a delve in the trunk and I'd taken supplies like an old khaki sleeping bag, some cans of cola and a multi-pack of crisps, as well as a torch and a hunting knife. I'd wrapped them all in some waterproof tarpaulin I'd found in Uncle Kev's garage. If Mam and Dad had noticed me gone, they'd've either thought I was at Uncle Kev's or not cared anyway so it was easy to come and go without being noticed.

Andrew was never there at night, but he'd come and find me first thing in the morning. The first time, he woke me up with a sloppy lick across me face. I'd been so tired I dreamed me nana was spitting into a stinky hanky and wiping me face with it. I hate it when nanas do that – it was really a relief to realise it was only a dog's slobbery tongue.

After the day I'd had, I knew I'd be too angry to sleep at home so I headed to me little den in the quiet woods and bunked down for the night. I didn't think life could get any worse than it was. How little I knew.

* JAMES *

We didn't go to the fair that night. Mum was really upset when she saw my busted nose. Ahmed's mum came over as soon as she heard and tried to persuade Mum to go to the police, but she refused, saying she "couldn't do that to Julie". She went really weird and sent Ahmed and me up to bed while all the grown-ups talked downstairs late into the night.

The next morning, while we were having breakfast, mum started talking about how some people have hard lives and we should appreciate what we have. I didn't understand what she meant. I'd been upset when I was first told about the changes our family would make, but I'd never complained since we'd moved here. I loved our new life. Mum said that was good, but we should be kind to others even if they didn't always seem to deserve kindness. Surely she didn't mean Greg Carlton? Not after he'd just bust my nose for no reason. That would be crazy talk.

That night we did go to the fair and it was fantastic. Dad came on some crazy rides with us while Mum stayed at the bottom refusing to look because she was too scared. Mum made me go on the teacups with Rosie and Ahmed jumped in too. Now that's a true friend who doesn't care how un-cool he looks. By the time we'd stuffed our faces with a mixture of hot dogs, candy floss and toffee apples and walked home, it was really late. Dad said we'd had enough excitement for one night and we should go straight to bed as it was school the next day and normally Ahmed wouldn't have been allowed to stay over on a school night. We promised we'd go straight to bed and straight to sleep, but all the sugar in our system was keeping us awake.

After Mum and Dad had gone to sleep, we were still wide awake and we couldn't resist sneaking down to the den again to look out for our little clan. I'd never blatantly ignored my parent's instructions before and the adrenaline still hadn't left us from all the rides and all the sugar.

We waddled down the garden looking like the meat in a sausage roll with our pastry duvets wrapped around us. Stealthily, we climbed the tree, pulling ourselves up into the den. It was so exciting. Without Dad with us, it felt like we were true spies on a real undercover operation. We took turns looking through the binoculars, waiting to see what would happen tonight.

CHAPTER 9

* GREG *

After the carry on with Kyle and the horse the day before, I'd been in no mood for the fair. I'd stayed in the woods that Saturday night and then the next night as well. I'd moved me den again, this time, a bit closer to the edge of the woods, not far from Andrew's fox hole, but not so close I was in any danger. Andrew always seemed to come from that side of the woods and I felt safer being a bit closer to him. I had some wild idea in me head that if anything happened to me, Andrew would appear from nowhere and fight off owt attacking me.

I tried to settle down to sleep in me tent, but I just felt too miserable. I couldn't stop thinking about everything that had happened the day before.

I lay there, replaying the scene in me head. Me kid brother flying through the air, landing face down in horse crap and them kids laughing. Laughing at me family.

When I'd got Kyle home I'd told me dad that I'd sorted the kids at the park but he hadn't said nowt about it to me. He'd just turned to me mam and screamed at her for not knowing where her kids were. He talked about us like we weren't even there. I'd felt worthless.

I lay there trying not to feel cold, thinking about me crap life, when I thought I heard sommat.

Quietly, I stood up. Half dozy with tiredness, me eyes were drawn towards Andrew's fox hole. I could hear a scuffling noise coming from inside it. Me senses became sharp and me head started tingling. I immediately wished I hadn't camped so near. I'd never been close to a big, wild animal before.

Just like on that first day when I met the squirrel, I froze to the spot and held me breath. Was I gunna be tomorrow's news: Loser in Woods is Ripped to Shreds by Pack of Wild Foxes? I hesitated. *Should I run now before it comes out to get a head start, or stay totally still and hope it doesn't notice me?* Too late to run – I could see the evil glint of a pair of shiny eyes, and they were staring straight at me.

* JAMES *

Ahmed and I wrapped our duvets tightly round us and propped our elbows on our pillows. We looked out over the garden, over the hedge and through the gap in the trees to the badger sett, taking turns with the infrared binoculars, waiting for Mr Blake to make his appearance. We were getting used to their routines now. Mr Blake always crawled out first. He would have a sniff around, do a little reverse and then come forward with his family in tow. We were pretty sure the babies were supposed to come out last, but often they were too impatient and would scramble over their mum and aunty in their excitement to go exploring.

Sure enough, right on cue, out crept Mr Blake. Unexpectedly, he froze with his head turned away from us. I moved the binoculars to see what he'd seen. There was the shape of a man in the woods. And he was looking directly at Mr Blake. "Ahmed," I whispered, "there's somebody in the woods." Neither the man, nor Mr Blake moved a muscle.

Then quick as a flash Mr Blake spun back to the sett and at the same time the man let out a loud squeal and ran straight towards us.

* GREG *

The eyes glowed and locked onto mine. I held me breath. The tingling in me head was the worst I'd ever felt and there were so many bubbles in front of me eyes, I couldn't see properly. Me skin felt like it had static electricity all over it and I could feel me body beginning to shake. This was it. This was the end.

The animal made a sudden movement and all me breath came out as a high-pitched squeal as I ran as fast as I could towards a small house I could just make out against the sky line.

The next thing I knew I was on the floor. Me foot had gone down a hole and I had the sharpest, hottest pain in me ankle. I knew straight away I'd broken it. I began to panic. Now the creature could have me. How could I get away? I called out in terror for somebody, anybody to help me.

"It's okay," soothed a voice right next to me, "my friend's gone to get his dad."

"There's an animal," I gasped, "it's gunna get me."

"The animal has gone, and here comes Mr Taylor."

To my embarrassment, I realised whose house I'd tried to run towards. It was those stupid kids and that ridiculous looking man. Then I remembered I'd head-butted his son and I was trapped by me leg as he was striding towards me. The adrenaline that hadn't had time to leave me body from the fright with the wild animal rose inside me again as I looked around for a weapon to defend meself.

"Stay still, son," muttered Mr Taylor as he looked at me leg. Perhaps he didn't know who I was in the dark. "You've badly twisted your ankle."

"It's *broken*," I snapped at him.

"Well let's see if we can help you up. While your foot's still down that hole it's going to be hurting."

Mr Taylor helped me up and although me ankle really stung, I realised it probably wasn't broken. Not yet anyway. Not until Mr Taylor recognised me, then I'd be for it.

"Will your mum and dad be wondering where you are Greg?" asked Mr Taylor.

So they knew. "Yes," I lied, in the hope that Mr Taylor wouldn't dare do anything if he thought me parents knew where I was.

"Good, well let's get you in the house and you can have a hot chocolate while my wife rings your mum and we wait for them to come and collect you."

Just then Andrew came bounding over and jumped up and licked me face.

"Stay down, Sam!" ordered Mr Taylor.

So he was *their* dog. Strangely, I felt betrayed. I'd thought of Andrew as me own dog. I purposely hadn't wanted to think about where he went when he wasn't with me. I began to feel like an idiot. A hopeless idiot. To make things worse, the same boys who'd seen me kid brother land in horse crap had now heard me scream like a girl and seen me fall down a hole. "There was a big wild fox after me," I tried to explain.

"It wasn't a fox, it was a badger," scoffed James. His dad shot a look at him and he went red and looked down at the floor.

* JAMES *

I couldn't believe what I'd just blurted out. My dad had warned me never to tell anyone about the secret badger family and I'd just told my worst enemy. If ever I could have a superpower I would choose the power to turn back time.

Dad was explaining to Greg that he had nothing to worry about, that the badger was more afraid of him than he was of it. Shame washed over me and I felt the hot prick of tears in the back of my eyes. I went out of the room and Ahmed followed me. Dad called me back but I couldn't face him. I climbed into bed and cried myself to sleep.

The next morning Dad said he had good news, "We've invited Greg to watch the badgers with you."

I glanced at Ahmed. He looked as horrified as me, "What if Greg tells others about the badgers? They'll be in danger."

"He already knows about the badgers. We can't undo that," Dad reasoned.

I felt myself go red in frustration.

"However, we can educate him about them. Help him to understand that they're not just disposable things to be destroyed or vicious beasts to be hated. If he sees them playing and grooming each other, maybe he'll develop empathy for them and end up loving our little clan as much as we do."

"But Dad, it's Greg Carlton. He's nasty and he's a bully. I don't want to spend *any* time with him. I don't want him coming here and I certainly don't want to have him in my den."

"Son. Sometimes you have to look deeper than the surface. I know you're worried, but trust me – there are times in life when you have to be brave, you have to do things that make you uncomfortable, because somebody else needs a chance. Sometimes, some people just need to be cut some slack son."

Then Dad laughed and winked at us, "Anyhow, don't worry, Greg won't be telling anyone about the badgers, otherwise you might let people see the CCTV of him squealing in fear."

"What CCTV? We don't have any CCTV."

Dad just smiled and winked.

"Oh! But…" I didn't know what else to say. I didn't want Greg here, but it was my fault he knew about the badgers and Dad had made up his mind.

Greg came over the next night with a miraculously healed ankle, climbed into the den and watched the badgers with us. Despite being determined to hate him, I couldn't resist showing off all my knowledge about badgers. "These are the enigmatic creatures of the night." I quoted my dad.

"Why night time?" he asked. "Why don't they come out in the day when they can see better? They're not like rabbits that need to hide – they could fight owt they saw."

"Well you're right that they *can* fight, but they don't actually *want* to fight. You see, they're peaceful creatures that don't want to be bothered."

I watched as Greg mulled over what I'd told him. "But if they're peaceful, why do they have massive long claws? And they go around killing animals."

"The claws are for digging," I told him. "They're powerful diggers, in fact their name comes from a French word for digging. You're right – they can easily kill animals if they need to eat, but they mostly live on earthworms. Thousands of them."

Greg furrowed his brow and I was worried he might think I was lying to make a fool of him. Quickly, I grabbed one of the books we'd brought back from the library. "Look!" I showed him. "It tells you all sorts of interesting things. Like, for instance, they leave little piles of poo called latrines dotted around the perimeter of their area so other badgers know to stay out."

"What? Like a poo fence?" He stared hard at my face, then he nodded. "Yer know some weird stuff mate." I breathed a sigh of relief and we turned back to spying on the badgers. As Greg watched the badger cubs tumbling over each other I realised that this was the first time I'd seen Greg Carlton smile. He didn't look half as scary when he smiled. I wondered how he could be so angry and miserable so much of the time. It must be depressing.

Over the weeks and months that followed, he became a regular visitor to our tree den. He loved watching the babies playing with their mum, and then he would look sad and I almost began to feel sorry for him, but then he wouldn't hand the binoculars over and snarled at me each time I tried to make a grab for them. So, a strange and slightly uneasy friendship developed between Greg, Ahmed and me. We didn't really want him there, but it was nice to have someone to teach all about badgers, someone who seemed to be just as genuinely interested and excited about them as we were. We never dared ask him why he'd been in the woods that night.

CHAPTER 10

* GREG *

It's strange how different people are when you get to know them properly. I never bothered with James or Ahmed when I was at primary school. Partly because they were two years below me, but mostly they just weren't the type of kids I'd hang out with. Ahmed was alright and his dad was cool, but James was a bit wet looking and had a weird looking dad.

That night when I thought I was about to be eaten alive by a fox was the oddest night ever for me. James' mam and dad sat with me for ages in their kitchen. I'd not seen Mrs Taylor before, she was fairly ordinary on first glance – mousey brown shoulder length hair and brown eyes, average height, average weight, nowt special. But when she spoke, you couldn't help but notice the kind look she has on her face. I don't know if it was the roundness of her eyes, or her wide mouth, or her rosy cheeks, but she just looked... I dunno... *kind*. You know when you were little and lost your mam at the supermarket? She'd be the one who'd hold your hand and take you to Security.

Apparently, James' mam used to be best friends with me mam. I never knew. When she went off to phone Mam, Mr Taylor made me the tastiest hot chocolate ever and I realised I hadn't even eaten that day until then. I'd thought that as soon as Mrs Taylor had gone, Mr Taylor would start shouting at me or hitting me, but instead he did the strangest thing. He invited me to hang out with James and Ahmed to watch the badgers. He told me that if Andrew (or Sam as he called him) liked me then I couldn't be a bad person really. Not deep down. It didn't make any sense. I'd hit their son, they'd caught me hanging around in the woods near their house but they were treating me as though I was a family friend. Weird.

I went round the next evening because I didn't wanna look like I was scared, but I *was* scared. I thought it might be a trick. Even though it was after tea time, it was still dead warm. It'd been too hot all day but now there was a bit of a breeze so it was just nice. James answered the door and invited me in. His dad stood behind him and the way he was pressing his fingers into James' shoulders I could tell James wasn't happy about the arrangement.

James led the way to the bottom of the garden where there was a big tree. As we got closer, I could see an old ladder leaning against the trunk. James climbed up first and I followed. Above our heads were some planks of wood making a kind of ceiling. James reached up and pushed one section and a square about the same size as a manhole cover flipped open, just big enough for us to squeeze through.

When I stuck me head through the hole, I couldn't believe what I saw. It was a proper treehouse. There were cushions and sleeping bags, and a stack of books and a little pully system to pull heavy items up into the den. Natural ledges formed by branches that it had been built round were being used as little shelves to hold packets of crisps and biscuits and drinks. There was even a walkie-talkie and a pair of expensive looking binoculars. It would've been dark in there except they'd strung some Christmas lights that gave a cosy orange glow and there was a low, wide rectangle cut out along one wall, just above where the sleeping bags and pillows were set out.

I stared out the window and straight onto the woods. This must've been where James and Ahmed were when the fox, no the badger, chased me. That's how they saw me.

After a few awkward moments, James was strangely chatty telling me all about how they'd built the den and how long it had taken and why they wanted to spy on the badgers. It all seemed a bit odd. Why would the family be so forgiving? What were they really up to? I watched James closely. He'd been telling me some weird stuff about badgers not being aggressive and only eating worms. It all sounded made up to me. If he was taking the mick, I didn't care where we were, I'd sort him out and make sure he never tried owt clever like that again. I felt me body begin to stiffen as I tried to control meself, but he was really pushing me. Suddenly, he grabbed a book and started blabbering about little crap piles that badgers leave out. He was definitely taking the mick.

"There," he pointed. "They're called latrines."

I didn't wanna look in case it was a trick.

"There," he said again.

Without turning me head, I glanced where he was pointing. There was a photograph in the book, of badger crap with an arrow pointing *latrines*.

"It's important we know where their setts are so we can keep an eye on them," James was saying, "They're protected by law and our badger clan is protected by us."

I began to realise that they thought the badger sett was the most important thing in their lives. A strange family, but I couldn't help feeling a bit jealous. I mean for a start the mam was sober and even though the dad was still the most bizarre looking bloke I ever saw, he was also real funny and he'd made the most awesome den in their tree. I tried to imagine me own dad doing something like that with me and realised he'd rather be down the pub or watching football with his mates.

I suddenly thought, if me dad knew I was hanging around with a couple of posh kids from primary school he'd think I'd gone soft and I'd never hear the last of it. Me mates and me cousins would be the same. Thing is, I *wanted* to come again.

I looked at James and Ahmed, they were laid on their fronts, Ahmed had the binoculars and was telling James what he could see. I pushed James' shoulder, "Listen here, don't take it the wrong way or nowt, but I don't want no-one knowing I come here."

James turned a bit red. "Thank goodness for that, I don't want anyone knowing you're coming here either."

I had to laugh. I hadn't thought of it from his point of view. He was probably embarrassed hanging out with someone like me off the estate.

I looked out the window again towards the hole. James had said badgers only come out at night, but I was sure I could see something moving. Ahmed and James looked too. They were amazed. The badgers had come out to play in broad daylight. The three of us lay there on the sleeping bags watching them. They were so funny. One of them kept jumping on top of a tree stump.

"That's Belinda," Ahmed whispered. "Her favourite game is King of the Castle, but Brock, her brother, hates losing." Sure enough, Brock jumped onto the tree stump and pushed her off.

"You've got names for them all?" I asked.

"Yes, otherwise we get confused about which ones we're talking about."

"How can you tell which is which?"

"Erm… well we can't always," Ahmed admitted. "If Belinda and Brock are next to each other we can see that Brock is a bit bigger and Mr Blake is the biggest adult, but we never know if we're looking at Mrs Blake or Aunty Blake. We can tell by the way they behave though. Aunty Blake never plays for long and gets naggy really quickly, we think she's probably quite old, whereas Mrs Blake will always have a wrestle with them. She's always trying to groom them too, but Belinda and Brock keep running away."

"Belinda's funnier than Brock," James added. "She's smaller so when they're wrestling Brock can win easily, so instead she does Ninja moves."

"Ninja moves?"

"Well we call them her Ninja moves, she rolls

one way and then just as Brock's about to land on her she spins round with super speed and he usually lands flat on his face. We're sure she laughs at him."

The weird chittering noises they were making kinda sounded like chuckling. It would quickly turn into growls if one of them went too far though.

After about twenty minutes of play, the whole family – or clan as James told me – went back into their hole and we all went inside to tell Mr and Mrs Taylor what we'd seen. Mr Taylor was real surprised to hear that the badgers had come out in daylight and joked that they must've been putting on a special welcome display just for me.

I started visiting more and more. Sometimes if I arrived early enough they'd give me dinner, which Mr Taylor made – another weird thing about him. The first night I had dinner with them, it was minced meat and dumplings. "This is proper nice," I told him. They all burst out laughing. I looked at them. I couldn't work out what was so funny – *were they laughing at me?*

"I suppose it is nice compared to his attempt at Lasagne," laughed Mrs Taylor giving him a playful nudge.

"Well who knew that you couldn't finish the layers with pasta on top?" Mr Taylor said.

"Evidently, you."

James turned to me. "The top was awful, it was crunchy and chewy at the same time. We had to leave it and only eat the bottom of the Lasagne."

"It still wasn't as bad as the time he tried to make gravy with fish oil though." said Mrs Taylor.

"That was bad," admitted Mr Taylor, "But that

was a genuine accident, I picked up the wrong sauce."

"You'd been on the sauce, was the problem." said Mrs Taylor.

"Aye that as well," he said, giving her a playful punch to the ribs.

I laughed along with them, but the sound of all those different meals made me feel jealous. I didn't tell them I'd been living off microwave meals and pizzas for as long as I could remember.

Weeks went by and the weather began to turn cold. James had told me that we wouldn't see as much activity from the badgers over the winter months and I started to worry 'cos I knew I wouldn't have the excuse to visit so often, especially as Mrs Taylor worried about us all getting cold lying still in the den for so long each time.

Often, when I left their house, I would pretend to go home and then double back and sneak into the woods for the night. I felt safe knowing their house wasn't far away, and I still hated going home. Winter would soon put a stop to that though. How would I cope with home if I had to stay every night?

* * * * *

I was determined to stay one last time in the woods before winter set in proper. One last night of freedom before I was trapped in the prison cell of me miserable home.

Earlier in the evening, we'd been lying in the den looking for badgers as normal. Mr Taylor didn't stay long 'cos it was too cold so he went in the house making the excuse of getting us all hot chocolates. We stayed looking for about an hour but the badgers didn't come out, it must've been too cold for them, so we climbed down the tree trunk and went into the kitchen. I was feeling happy. I always did at their house.

Me mind was drifting back to the first time I ever visited. I'd always imagined them to have a massive modern house on the Manor Estate, but I was surprised to see they were crammed, into this tiny little cottage. It's smaller than our house. Thing is though, theirs is warm and clean and homely. From the outside the cottage looks real old, but you can see they've done loads to it to make it pretty. Mr Taylor has cut the grass real short and painted the front fence white like in olden day pictures. They've loads of pots and hanging baskets with flowers in, but you can still tell it's just a little old cottage.

You step into a porch first, which is absolutely crammed with shoes and coats and wellies and an old wooden box with hats, gloves and scarves bursting out. From the porch you step straight into their living room. You're always greeted immediately by a nice smell. Sometimes it's dinner or hot chocolate, sometimes it's the clean smell of bleach, or sometimes it's fresh flowers that Mr Taylor picks for his missus straight from the garden. The living room has two, two-seater sofas squeezed either side of a real fire with proper flames. There are pictures hanging on the walls showing happy family scenes of them all climbing a big hill or making sand castles on the beach or just generally being together having a good time. Some of the decoration is a bit naff, like the big flowery wallpaper in the living room, but it suits them. They're a bizarre, odd-looking bunch who don't quite fit in, but they're fun and happy and I like them.

I was enjoying the warmth of the hot chocolate as it slid down me throat, but I was beginning to feel sad as well 'cos I knew this would be the last time I'd be visiting until probably the spring.

Mr Taylor offered us one of his freshly baked cakes. They tasted okay, but they were always flat and heavy and a bit soggy so he used to try to hide that by smearing a ton of icing on top and then putting a giant chocolate button on top of that. We had one each and then Mr Taylor told Ahmed and James they needed to tidy away before bed. I knew it was time for me to go but I hung around a bit longer and ate another cake to buy time. Eventually, Mr Taylor said I'd need to be off 'cos me parents would worry. We both knew they wouldn't, but it was his polite way of telling me to go, so off I went.

Once I was far enough away from their house I crept round the field behind it and doubled back to the woods. Even in the dark, I now found it easy to find the tree where I always hid me supplies, but tonight there was a full moon lighting me way. It wasn't a nice yellow moon though, it was a ghostly silver one that kind of made the woods look spooky. I hesitated for a moment wondering whether I should just go home, but I knew this would be the last chance for a long time, so I pulled Uncle Kev's tarpaulin out of the hollow of the tree and rolled it out on the ground.

I was quick at putting up me makeshift tent now,

the tarpaulin was just long enough to lie under me sleeping bag, then reach up and over a low branch then down and back under the sleeping bag again, giving a triangle of protection against the weather. I wriggled in feet first feeling quite skilled at how effortless this had become. The tarpaulin had been out so long now it had weathered to the point that it just looked like an extension of the tree. I felt like a survival expert off the TV.

Me den was well hidden behind some thick brambles and down a bit of a dip, out of sight of the infrared binoculars. There were two reasons I never told the Taylors that I stayed here. One – Mrs Taylor actually cared about me and would definitely have stopped me from sleeping outside. Two – I was closer to the sett than James said we should be and I didn't want them to think badly of me. How mad that I cared what a little squirt like James thought. I didn't really understand why I cared. I just knew that I did.

I lay there half alert listening for the snuffling sounds of Mr Blake and his family. I hoped Andrew would come, I wanted the warmth of his body as much as the company, but he was usually locked in overnight – imprisoned in his home like I felt in my home. Although, when I thought about it, I realised he didn't see it as a prison. He loved his family and his family loved him. I wished he was here with me tonight though. I felt on edge, like sommat wasn't quite right. The moon was the wrong colour, there was no wind, no movement whatsoever. Even the screeching of an owl would be welcome right now. I burrowed down into me sleeping bag and tried not to think about nowt.

I'm not sure how long I was there thinking of Andrew and listening for Mr Blake. I'd reached that point between sleep and awake where you're not sure if you're dreaming or not. I must've been dreaming, 'cos I could hear diesel engines yet I was in the woods.

CHAPTER 11

* JAMES *

The night it happened, Ahmed was staying over. We'd had a fairly uneventful night watching for Mr Blake, who'd had more sense than us and decided not to brave the cold night. Dad made us all his speciality hot chocolates and then Greg had gone home. I couldn't believe how friendly we all were these days. Greg would never say hi to us if he passed us in the street as it ruined his 'street-cred', but when he came here we all got on pretty well.

Both Mum and Dad had insisted that I either accept Greg as a friend who would watch badgers with us or we would no longer watch badgers. I was outraged initially, but we'd all reached a comfortable understanding together. In fact, I'd say we got on better than that. As I watched Greg walk away that night, I felt a pang of guilt not inviting him to stay over with Ahmed and me. I wondered if he had any friends. He never mentioned any.

Mum said we could have half an hour playing on the computer before bed, so we were watching funny animal compilations on YouTube. Eventually, after an hour, our loud laughter gave us away and Dad switched the Wi-Fi off. This was supposed to be our signal to get to sleep but who goes to sleep on a sleepover?

Instead of getting dressed for bed, we decided to wait until Mum and Dad had gone to sleep, put a few extra layers of clothing on, then sneak down to the treehouse to stay out one last night. Mum would go mad if she knew because the night was already cold. It's always more exciting when it's not allowed though.

Carefully, we crept down the stairs with our duvets wrapped around us. Sam wanted to come out with us but he'd only run back to the house after half an hour, scratching at the door to be let in and give us away, so I bribed him with a biscuit and he ate it in his bed. We tiptoed down the garden looking like two giant, grotesque maggots and clambered up into the den.

Once in the den, Ahmed began to tell me some of his mum's spy stories. I loved these stories although I still didn't believe that she was really a spy, but I never let on. He was telling me about an international terrorist called Mally O'Mally.

"I've never heard of him," I whispered.

"No, you wouldn't, he is so dangerous he has to be kept out of the news, because MI5 don't want other terrorists to copy his ideas. He is classified as one of the top most dangerous villains because he's not only filled with hate, he's also highly intelligent. Usually, it's not too difficult to track most members of terrorist groups, but Mally O'Mally is so highly intelligent, not only has he managed to stay on the run and continue his terrorist operations for twenty years, he has also recruited twenty others who are also untraceable."

Ahmed went on to explain that Mally O'Mally wasn't even his real name. The day Ahmed's mum had captured him they had been trying to track a man whose name was either Mally something or something Mally. He escaped from custody less than a week later with no-one ever discovering his real name and the nickname Mally O'Mally had stuck.

Ahmed said nobody ever heard from Mally O'Mally again. There were rumours he'd been killed by one of his own men, but Ahmed's mum didn't believe that could happen. He was far too clever for that. She was convinced he was just watching and waiting for the right time to return. And when he did it would be a catastrophe for the public.

As always, Ahmed's stories gave me the creeps. Mally O'Mally was a big man, yet he could disappear in crowds. He always wore a flat cap to cover a distinguishing scar over his eyebrow but nobody knew how he got the scar. He never ever spoke – nobody had heard his voice. Even when he was shot in the back of the leg the day Ahmed's mum captured him, he hadn't screamed, hadn't panted. He just turned and looked with a look so cold, Ahmed's mum swore frost had appeared on the grass around him.

After Ahmed finished the story, I could feel the hairs standing up all over my body. I raised the binoculars to look for Mr Blake and drew some comfort from seeing him climbing out of his sett. Suddenly, Mr Blake froze then turned around and was gone in a flash. I looked and saw the figure of a man in the woods, and this time it definitely wasn't Greg Carlton. For a start, he was much bigger. And he was wearing a flat cap. He was looking directly towards us.

I signalled to Ahmed. Whoever it was, was not moving. They clearly didn't want to be seen. Then we saw torch lights further back in the woods and heard dogs barking. When I looked back the man had moved. "What's happening?" Ahmed asked.

The hair on the back of my neck stood straight and my ears felt like they were trying to move in the direction of the sounds coming from the woods. Dad says it's from the days when we could raise our hackles and push our ears back. I was sensing danger just like Mr Blake.

* GREG *

The diesel engines seemed to be getting louder. I opened me eyes and right in front of me was a pair of legs. A man's pair of legs. For a second I wondered why Mr Taylor would be in the woods and thought maybe I'd been caught, but Mr Taylor's legs were long and skinny. These were shorter and stockier. This was a stranger. I held me breath. He was facing away from me towards the Taylor's house. I had a bad feeling in me guts. Why was he there? The moon slid out from behind a cloud and reflected sommat shiny in his hand. *A knife?* I lay there trying to quieten me heartbeat. Whatever happened, the bloke mustn't know I was there. I didn't move.

The engines were getting louder and the man turned towards them with one hand raised. The engines stopped and I heard quiet raspy voices and muffled barking. About a dozen burly men joined the first man with spades and terriers.

I felt sick. Instantly, I knew what these men were here for. They were gunna dig Mr Blake and his family out for badger baiting.

I lay there, hoping a plan would pop into me brain, watching helplessly as the men searched for the sett. If I could get to Mr Taylor's he could help, but the men were between me and the house. They were already close to the sett and would find it very soon. There was nowt I could do except stay absolutely still and hope they didn't see me.

CHAPTER 12

* JAMES *

As I stared at the man I became aware of the sound of engines. The strange man turned and signalled and the engines stopped. Men's voices drifted to us and we could hear dogs yapping.

"They're looking for the badgers," whispered Ahmed.

I nodded. "We've got to tell Dad." As we turned we heard a shout and another man came forward. The moon revealed the identity of the second man: Greg's dad.

Silently, we climbed down the ladder and crawled towards the hedge keeping our heads well below eye level.

"I can't believe Greg has brought badger baiters to our sett," I growled. "I can't believe we were stupid enough to trust him." Suddenly, it all fell into place. A tough kid like him wanting to spend time with unpopular kids like us. Asking me so many questions about badgers and listening carefully to all my explanations. And we'd let him drink Dad's hot chocolate and allowed him to spend time chatting with my lovely mum. Now the badgers were going to suffer because of him. Because he'd betrayed them. I hated him.

I pounced into the air ready to run at Greg's dad, but Ahmed grabbed me by my clothes and dragged me back down.

"Shhh!" his eyes glistened with fury or excitement, I wasn't quite sure. "We need to have a plan." He was right of course. "I know a little about badger baiters. They'll only capture the badgers for now, bundling them very tightly in bags so they can't move and can't use their claws or jaws to escape. Then they'll throw them into cages in the back of the Land Rovers and take them somewhere else for the fighting. We're just kids, we can't fight them, and if we run to your dad's and phone the police, by the time they're here the badger baiters will be long gone. Anyway, we can't run across your garden without the security lights coming on and lighting us up like stars on a stage. These are all knuckle-heads, we've got to use our brains, that's the only way to beat them."

The dogs' yapping had changed. It was sharper and urgent. They'd got Mr Blake's scent. I felt sick. How frightened would the badgers be right now? Especially the little babies Brock and Belinda. What would Mrs Blake do? I imagined her leading the youngsters up each escape tunnel one by one and being chased back down by a vicious terrier. She would protect the babies by hiding them behind her and attack each terrier head on until there were too many for her to fight. She would either fight to her death protecting her babies or lead them up the only escape hole left open and the men would capture her and her babies in their sinister sacks. The terror they'd feel would be nothing compared to when they're taken away to a fighting pit where the big dogs would be waiting for them…

Tears sprang to my eyes threatening my vision, and I hurriedly wiped them away. "Okay. What shall we do then?"

"Let them have their fun and work off their energy with their spades and their shouting. Let them think they've succeeded. While they're distracted and making tonnes of noise, we sneak up behind the Land Rovers and hide. Wait until the badgers are in the vehicles, then just as they're about to set off, we sneak up and unbolt the cages without anyone seeing. They won't know they've lost them until they've reached their destination and by then it will be too late.

"One more thing – if either of us gets caught, the other one must get away and find help. No matter how bad it looks or sounds, we cannot risk both of us being caught. To leave a comrade to the enemy goes against everything I believe in, but thinking tactically there are too many of them against us." He stared intently at me. "Agreed?"

I nodded. "Agreed."

Strangely, I didn't feel frightened, only determined. Greg had bullied me and others for long enough, but bullying animals was a step too far.

Taking our trust and using it against Mr Blake and his family was beyond despicable. Quietly, Ahmed and I wriggled on our bellies behind the hedge until we reached the corner of the garden where there was a sizeable gap which Sam had widened. We slid through and ran along the edge of the field towards the woods.

We circled wide, making as little noise as possible, although every crunch of leaves and snap of twigs seemed louder than the men's cheers and shouts. Among the sound of the men and dogs, we could hear the badgers' hoarse screaming. The sound tore at my ears and it took all my self-control not to just run straight in and try to attack the men. Ahmed was right though. We couldn't beat them with brute force. We had to follow our plan.

Eventually, we reached the Land Rovers and as Ahmed had predicted, there were cages in the back. We sneaked backwards, further into the undergrowth and waited, trying to block out the images of snarling teeth and petrified baby badgers.

I imagined what my mum would do if a gang of strange men were surrounding our house, ready to attack me and my little sister. I imagined her fear and rage. I imagined my meek and mild mum stretching up to her full five feet and four inches, baring her teeth and attacking with the strength of ten men. I knew for definite, my mum would fight to her death to protect Rosie and me.

After an age of whooping, laughing and shouting the men came stumbling back with four tightly bound, bulging sacks. Each was roughly thrown into a cage with no concern whatsoever for the frightened creatures inside. Doors were slammed shut, then the men all congregated around the front of the vehicles, smoking cigarettes and congratulating each other on a job well done.

I watched as Ahmed slid as soundless as a shadow to the first Land Rover. Silently, he opened the back door just enough to slide his arm in, then he glided the cage bolt back without opening the cage door. If he had, the badger might sense the opening and make a noise, giving them all away. But with the bolt slid back, the cage door would fall open only when the Land Rover drove off, and although the badger might be bruised and hurt as it fell out in its bag, anything was better than the brutal death it would receive at the jaws of multiple vicious fighting dogs in a badger baiting pit.

Ahmed stepped sideways, staying in the shadows cast by the moon and repeated his drill. The badgers weren't moving at all, although they were making muffled, panicky growling noises. Ahmed was already at the third Land Rover when he motioned for me to open the one that was nearest. I copied Ahmed and slid along in the dark shadows. As I quietly slipped the bolt open, I could see that this bag had two smaller lumps in it – it was the babies. They weren't bound as tightly and were able to wriggle a little. Just as I slid the bolt back, one of them knocked the cage door which, to my horror, flung against the Land Rover rear door with a loud CLACK!

Instantly, all the torches shone our way and my heart stopped.

"Sommat's wrong." shouted one of the men as

they all ran to the back of the Land Rovers. As
Ahmed looked at me I could see the same fear in his
eyes that I was sure showed in mine. We turned and
ran. Blind panic gave us super speed. Immediately,
the men took up the chase. If we could just run fast
enough, we could hide from them, deeper in the
woods.

Ahmed sprinted off into the shadows and I had trouble keeping up, but the sound of big men crashing after us spurred me on faster and faster. We were running, jumping, ducking, and swerving. Brambles clawed at our legs, branches took sweeps at our heads, and the ground seemed to make itself as uneven as possible. Still we ran. Still the men kept crashing after us.

Fear consumed me. What would they do if they caught us? Would we face the same horrors as the badgers being thrown into a pit with killer dogs? My legs pounded hard into the uneven ground, I ducked under another branch, jumped over another rock, swerved around another tree. Ahmed seemed to be invincible as he ducked and dived, as graceful as a stag travelling at an immense speed.

The crashing of the big men behind me seemed to be getting louder. I thought I was already going my fastest, but somehow, I managed to pick up even greater speed. A branch ripped across my face. Any other time the pain would have crippled me, but this was nothing compared to what a dog would do to me if the men caught us.

If I could just keep running, surely the men would give up soon. I couldn't seem to get enough air into my lungs, I was panting with my mouth wide, running and running. They were smokers, surely it wouldn't be long before they were out of breath and would give up chasing us?

Then I heard the dogs. They'd joined in the chase. There was no chance we could out run them.

Another branch whipped me across the face making my vision blurry. I wiped my eye as I ran and suddenly realised that Ahmed was out of sight. He'd disappeared. We were better off splitting up anyway, if one of us got caught the other could go for help. I pushed myself harder. The sound of the men seemed to be getting more distant, then I hit a tree stump and smashed face down into the ground.

Two terriers lunged at my legs and began attacking my trainers. I kicked out as fast and as hard as I could, desperately scrabbling trying to get back up and run. It was too late. The men were on me. Rough hands dragged me to my feet. I kicked and flailed my arms around, making as much noise as possible so they wouldn't be able to hear Ahmed still running. Wherever he was.

* GREG *

I just stood there, stunned. It was like I'd been thrown into a movie. When the men started digging out the badgers, I was still frozen to the spot, then I heard a twig snap to the left of me. To me complete and utter amazement, I saw James and Ahmed wriggling on their bellies through the undergrowth like a pair of bad cartoon Rambos. I didn't know if they were being very brave or very stupid. They snuck between the trees seeming to make a massive amount of noise but luckily the dogs' barking was louder. Then they disappeared.

I stayed where I was, hoping the men would go without finding me. The badgers were making a screaming sound. It made me head tingle so bad it was hurting, me skin was itching all over and I kept seeing flashes of light in front of me eyes. I'd never heard this noise they were making before. When they were play-fighting they sometimes screamed at each other, but this was different. This was raw and real. *Real* fear. *Real* terror.

Each time the men caught a badger they grabbed it by the tail and swung it upside down into a bag, fastening it up so tight it couldn't move. Then they half-carried, half *dragged* the poor things back towards the Land Rovers. They were coming closer and closer to me tent. Like an idiot, I shut me eyes. Then their voices faded and they'd passed without noticing me. I took in a great big gulp of air, realising I'd been holding me breath again. The men chucked the badgers still in their sacks, into cages in the back of the Land Rovers then stood around the front smoking and talking.

There was no mistaking one of the men. It was me dad. I shouldn't't've been surprised. I knew me dad was a badger baiter but I'd never really thought nowt of it before. That's what he had Rocky for and he usually made a bit of money on the betting. Me dad hated badgers. He said they were vicious killers and people should be glad him and his mates get rid of them. They were doing the public a service. He said they deserved to be ripped apart 'cos they'd jump at the chance to do the same to a baby or a small child if they found one in the woods. Tonight, for the first time ever, I felt totally ashamed of me dad.

Suddenly there was a load of shouting, all the men ran to the back of the Land Rovers then they all went running off into the woods. I realised straight away they must've seen Ahmed and James. *Now what should I do? Should I chase after them and try to help Ahmed and James? Should I run the opposite way and tell Mr Taylor?* I recognised a distressed chittering sound from the back of one of the Land Rovers. *The badgers. What should I do?*

I stood there trying to get the guts to approach the Land Rovers. What if one of the men was still there? What if the men came back? I knew I needed to rescue the badgers but I didn't think I could. I didn't dare. I might get caught. I stayed where I was.

The men's voices were beginning to fade into the trees as they ran further and further away after James and Ahmed. If I was going to rescue the badgers, this would be the perfect time. Still, I stood there. Me legs refused to move. I wanted to rescue them, I really did, but I just couldn't. I didn't dare.

And at that moment, I suddenly realised the truth about meself – I'd thought I was tough, but I wasn't. I wasn't tough at all. When it came to it and I had to do sommat real brave, I couldn't.

I thought back to when I was just a nipper, riding up to the park on me brand-new scooter. I used to think I was proper hard. I was proud of me shiny new ride, but I was even prouder of the terrified look on kids' faces when I rode at them, swerving with only a centimetre to spare. They knew me reputation and they used to burst into tears and run away. Thinking about it now, even at the time, part of me did feel bad. I mean, deep down I knew I wasn't a good person.

Until tonight, I thought I was the big man. Scared of nowt and scared of no-one, but everyone else scared of me. Yet there I was too frightened to move and the kids I used to frighten were the ones being brave.

The realisation dawned on me. Ahmed and James were tough. They'd just taken on a gang of hard-cases. They probably wouldn't live to tell the tale, but at least they'd had the guts to do sommat. Not like me. Too scared to move. When it came to it and I had to do something that took real guts, I couldn't. *I'm not brave, I'm just a coward. Nowt but a coward. No point denying it. It's true and there's nowt I can do about it.*

I stood there, ashamed and hating meself. I listened for the men but their voices had completely gone now, I could just hear the odd bark carried on the wind.

I stayed where I was. Frozen to the spot.

CHAPTER 13

* JAMES *

I have never been so terrified in my life. *They won't kill me, they can't kill me*, I kept repeating to myself in my head. *Killing animals is a sport to them, but killing a child is murder. They're not murderers. Ahmed has got away, he'll be able to go for help.* I knew I couldn't get away, but I kept fighting back, buying Ahmed as much time as possible.

One of the men grabbed my wrist with one hand and I clawed at him with my other hand. As he grabbed it, I sunk my teeth into his wrist. He yelped like a dog, then cursed and punched me in the stomach so hard I thought he must have put a hole in me. My breath was forced out and I couldn't breathe back in. I opened my mouth, trying to suck in air but I couldn't seem to make my lungs work. There was no oxygen left in my body and still I couldn't breathe. My legs went wobbly and I fell to the ground, still opening and closing my mouth like a stranded fish unable to suck in any air. Just as I thought I was about to pass out, my breath came back and I lay on the floor wheezing and panting. I was in a lot of pain, but relieved to be alive. For now.

Out the corner of my eye, I noticed the moonlight reflecting off something shiny and rippling. Water! I hoped and prayed Ahmed had seen it too. Somewhere in the depths of the old mill pond, I knew Ahmed would be watching and waiting for his chance to escape. I just hoped he would get help in time. Men who enjoyed watching animals rip each other apart were not the type of people I wanted to be spending any time with. My body began to tremble and I gulped for air.

* GREG *

I sank down to the ground. A coward. Helpless and hopeless.

Without warning, the tingling stabbed me in me head. It was stronger than I was used to and I nearly shouted out with the pain. Me skin felt like it was made of electric. At the same time the badgers weird, muffled, chittering noises got louder. The image of the badgers kept flashing up in front of me eyes and a strange feeling came over me body. I knew I had to help. From somewhere, I don't know where, I suddenly got the power to move and do the right thing. It felt like me mind wasn't mine. From nowhere I went into action-hero mode.

Quickly, I grabbed the knife from out me den and went to the back of the nearest Land Rover. The first bag was really big – maybe Mr Blake. I wanted to save him, but would he realise that or would he be so frightened that he'd attack me out of fear? We'd only ever watched the badgers from a distance through the binoculars. I'd never been up close to one before and I knew they could be dangerous when frightened.

I got an idea. I dragged the bag out onto the ground and scrambled into the cage. Then I leaned out and cut the tie off the end of the bag. From the safety of the cage, hanging over the edge of the Land Rover, I grabbed the other end of the bag and whipped it upwards causing the badger to tumble away from me. I instantly slammed the cage door shut with me on the inside and the badger safely on the ground on the outside.

"*Run,*" I hissed at Mr Blake, but he stayed still. Frozen to the spot. Me head was pounding, knocking me sick. *Not now,* I thought, *I don't need me head playing silly games now.* I didn't dare shout "Run" too loud so I shouted in me head at him. Mr Blake glanced at me then fled straight into the woods. I jumped down from the Land Rover and listened. I could hear the men shouting in the woods, they must be on their way back but they still seemed a long distance away.

As quick as I could, I went to the next Land Rover. Another big bag, probably Mrs Blake. I shoved her and her bag onto the floor and crawled into the cage to keep safe. I cut the end of the bag and whipped it off her. She stayed where she was. She was confused too.

"Run!" I looked for something to throw at her, but I only had me knife. If I kicked her she might turn round and bite me foot off. "Run, you idiot!" I half-shouted, half-whispered but mostly screamed inside me head, making the tingling and banging louder than ever. She looked at me once then scampered away. Me head was making me feel dizzy and even when I wasn't looking at the badgers, I could still see them in front of me eyes. I jumped down and listened again. From the excitement of the voices it sounded like they'd caught the lads. I had to work quick.

I pounced into Aunty Blake's cage, pushing her out and slashing the bag all at the same time, causing her to fall and tumble pretty badly.

Run, I screamed at her in me head. Immediately she ran off into the darkness without even looking at me. The men's voices were louder. They would be here soon.

I still needed to free the babies. They weren't bound up as tightly as the adults. This was gunna be harder. They were thrashing about and their claws were already starting to cut through the sacking, but they were mostly just thrashing against the side of the cage. How could I get hold of their sack to drag them out without being slashed by their claws? The men would be here any minute. I noticed a shovel leaning against the Land Rover. I threw me knife into Aunty Blake's now empty cage and grabbed the shovel instead. I rammed it against the babies hauling them out, probably cutting into them, but it couldn't be helped. Anything was better than them being ripped apart by a gang of dogs in a ring surrounded by me dad and his mates screaming and hollering.

I threw the shovel down and reached round to Aunty Blake's cage for the knife to slash the bag open. Without warning, a hand grabbed the back of me neck and smashed me face into the side of the Land Rover.

* JAMES *

The men dragged me through sharp brambles and over rocks back to the Land Rovers.

When we reached the vehicles, the first thing I saw was Greg Carlton. He was talking to his dad. He couldn't look at me. The men tied my wrists behind me and tied my legs together then they stuck some tape across my mouth and threw me into a cage, slamming the Land Rover door shut.

For one horrifying moment, I thought they were throwing me in with a badger, but the cage was empty. The badgers must have managed to fall out and escape while the men were chasing us. My moment of relief was short lived. If the badgers were gone and I was in the cage instead... was I about to replace the badgers and be thrown in a pit with huge murderous dogs?

I was petrified. These men clearly did not care about laws. They'd tied me up against my will, they'd punched me so hard I hadn't been able to breathe and they'd made me a prisoner. How far would they go? Sweat was dripping down my forehead and stinging my eyes. I had to calm down.

I couldn't panic because I only had my nose to breathe through. That thought was making me panic more. *Calm! Calm down! Ahmed was probably already calling the police. The men would be caught and I would be freed. Everything will be okay. Keep calm!*

Until my rescue, I needed to think of a plan to keep myself alive for as long as possible. If I was the one running for help and Ahmed was the one who was captured what would he do? He'd have a plan and it would begin with removing the tape from his mouth and the ties from his wrists and legs.

My arms were tied behind me so I began to rub my face against the side of the cage to scrape off the tape. I just needed to find one bit that wasn't stuck to my face and catch it on the cage side then I'd be able to peel it off. I rubbed my face in all directions like a cat rubbing its face against a person's legs. I was a bit more desperate than a cat though. I rubbed it up and down, left and right, clockwise and anti-clockwise. It all seemed to be smoothly pressed against my skin with no little edge to catch. I blew my cheeks out then sucked them in to try to loosen a tiny bit of the tape. It wouldn't budge. I fought down the feeling of panic which was trying to rise up in me again. *Okay, if I can free my hands, I will be able to remove the tape easily. Focus on the wrist ties.*

In films, the prisoner always found something sharp to rub their wrists against that would cut through the rope. This wasn't a film, though. For starters, it was too dark to be able to see clearly and secondly the space was too small to turn around in. I felt around with my fingers and immediately touched something cold and sharp. Something exactly like a knife. Surely not?

I wedged the handle into the mesh of the cage and started to saw the rope backwards and forwards over the blade. Each time I moved my wrists forwards, the handle became unwedged and the knife fell uselessly flat onto the cage floor so I had to keep wedging it back in again. I decided to only rub my wrists backwards not forwards. It would take twice as long, but it could work. I didn't know how long I had before the men would return. They were all gathered at the front of the Land Rovers, whispering urgently.

Finally, my wrists were free and I could hold the knife in my hand. I cut through the ropes around my ankles, then slowly peeled the tape from my mouth. It hurt, but I had bigger problems – the men were climbing into the Land Rovers. Quietly, I slid the bolt back on the cage. The cage door wouldn't open. It was pressed up against the Land Rover rear door.

Just then the door swung open, I felt an excruciating pain as I was dragged out by my hair. Looking up, I saw the silhouette of a man back lit by the moon. I felt his fist smash into my face and then everything faded into blackness.

CHAPTER 14

* GREG *

Whoever had smashed me face into the side of the Land Rover was now twisting me arm up me back so hard it was gunna snap. "Gerroff!" I shouted into the side of the Land Rover.

"Greg?" It was me dad. "What the hell are yer doing 'ere?"

"This is where I live now," I yelled back at him.

"What the hell are yer doing 'ere?" he repeated. "What are yer doing with the badgers? Have yer any idea how much planning has gone into this? There's fifty men waiting for us back at The Sheds. Expecting badgers, fighting, betting. How can I tell 'em it's me own son who's screwed us over?" He had his face so close to mine I could smell his sour breath and see the veins bulging on the side of his head. "I'm set to win a lot of money tonight. Rocky's at the top of his game. He could easily win against an adult badger tonight with another couple of dogs." He pounded his fist on the side of the Land Rover. "No-one's gunna bet on 'im against badger cubs. We need the big uns. The cubs are just gunna be used for training. They're an easy kill for a couple of young dogs new to the game."

I felt sick to me stomach. Those cute little baby cubs who love to play Hide and Seek and King of the Castle, who tumbled over their dad and nibbled at their mum: Brock and Belinda were going to be ripped to pieces by a pack of vicious, snarling dogs. "Leave off 'em Dad. Let 'em go. *Please.*"

"What? Have yer gone soft in the head? Yer worse than yer brother, an' he's dead soft. Me mates are coming back. Don't say owt. Don't let on yer was part of this stupid bloody cock-up. I'll never live it down, an' I don't know what they'll do to yer. I'll say yer was in the Land Rover all along 'cos yer wanted to watch the baiting."

I didn't wanna pretend to be part of the baiting gang, but I didn't know what me dad's mates would do to me neither. Me dad knew some pretty dodgy people, and I wasn't wanting to find out how dodgy they could be.

The men came back, dragging James with them. He looked at me, and I looked away. I couldn't look at him. I climbed into the front of me dad's Land Rover.

Me dad and the rest of the men gathered at the front of the vehicles. I couldn't make out who was who in the dark, but I could hear them arguing and see them smoking and looking round at me.

They'd thrown James into the cage in the back

and I could hear him wriggling around. The cubs had been chucked back into the cage in the Land Rover next to us and I could hear them chittering frantically and scratching helplessly against the metal sides. Me head was still buzzing. Eventually, the men came back to the Land Rovers. Me dad went to the back of ours. I heard him drag James out, swear, then throw him back in the cage. James didn't seem to be moving anymore.

"It's taken a lot of persuading, but the men think yer sneaked into me Land Rover at home 'cos yer want to get yer first taste of badger blood. We're going to The Sheds now. Yer gunna make a bet, yer gunna watch a fight, and yer gunna enjoy every minute of it. Right? 'Cos if yer let me down it's not just them yer need to be scared of. I'll be sorting yer out meself."

I sat quiet. What the hell? I didn't want to watch the babies or any other badgers being ripped apart. But I didn't want to be ripped apart by me dad and his mates neither. And why wasn't James moving anymore? What had he done to him? I wondered if me dad knew who he was. And I wondered what he was going to do to him next.

Dad turned the key and we set off with the rest of the Land Rovers.

I knew The Sheds. They were on Farmer Morris' land. Farmer Morris was someone who'd trade in poached stock – so long as it wasn't poached from his own land. He also dealt in stolen farm machinery, drugs, guns, anything that would make him some extra money. The Sheds were used for all sorts of illegal sports – underground boxing, badger baiting, cock-fighting. Locals never went near his farm 'cos he was a nutter and would drive his farm machinery at strangers. He wasn't just pretending neither. It's said he'd ploughed a hiker into his land when he was just a young man. He'd done time for it.

Me dad never said nowt to me as we drove along. He just gripped the wheel with one hand and smoked with the other looking dead ahead.

I sat there thinking about what'd just happened. Me head had stopped tingling and I could think more clearly. Me skin had calmed down too and I could see properly. Why did all these things happen if I was near Andrew or the badgers or even squirrels? Was I allergic to animals? If so I'd never heard of that kind of allergy before. I'd heard of breathing difficulties, spots and sneezing. Nobody had ever mentioned all the things that were happening to me. And when it happened it always seemed like I knew what the animals were thinking. Sometimes it was like I could even *see* what they were thinking. I'd never been wrong. As I thought about it, I realised I never used me voice with Andrew. I'd think something like, *let's go up the path*, and he'd start walking. Like he'd read me mind. Could animals understand me? Like Dr Dolittle? I almost laughed at the craziness of the idea. But I wasn't in a funny situation. I looked at me dad still gripping the wheel with one hand, smoking with the other. He still looked angry but the fag seemed to be calming him down a bit.

I thought about when I'd released the badgers from their sacks. I'd wanted them to run into the woods but when I'd spoken with me voice that hadn't done nowt. It was only when I shouted in me head making it worse, that they'd done what I'd wanted. They must be able to read me mind. Read me thoughts. Is that possible?

* * * * *

Eventually, we reached The Sheds. Me dad told me to stay in the Land Rover while he went to see Farmer Morris and tell him we had no adult badgers. From where I was sitting, I could see Farmer Morris wasn't none too pleased. There was a lot of shouting and arm waving, but luckily another group of men had dug up some badgers earlier in the week so they still had a few fights to bet on. I say luckily – luckily for me and luckily for me dad. Not luckily for the badgers. And not luckily for James, who still didn't seem to be moving. "James," I whispered. "*James*." I couldn't tell if he was just too scared to move, out cold, or dead.

Me dad came back and yanked me out of the Land Rover. "Remember – yer gunna enjoy every minute of this. Don't let me down," he growled.

I walked with him across the yard and into the first shed. The air was thick with cigarette smoke, stinging me eyes. The smell of sweat and beer hung heavy in the smoky air. Dad went up to someone he knew and introduced me. "Like father, like son." he proudly stated. I grinned, hoping it was convincing.

We went through to the main shed where they'd made a big square pit from pallets and straw bales, lined with corrugated tin sheeting to stop any frightened animals from escaping.

"Right son," me dad grinned, rubbing his hands

together, "this is gunna be a great night. Pick a dog and make a bet." I looked to where he was pointing. A group of men stood together with their fighting dogs. These were the ones that were gunna be fighting badgers tonight. Dad went and grabbed Rocky off his mate who'd been holding him.

"I'll bet on Rocky, Dad."

"Good lad, good lad." I'd never seen me Dad so happy in ages. He was so into convincing everyone that I wanted to be here, he'd convinced himself too. He was proud as punch of me, just like he used to be in me younger days. He had a skip in his step as he made his way towards a bloke in a trilby hat, who was taking everyone's bets while puffing on a cigar.

Some of me dad's mates recognised me and came over. They were all real pleased to see me and were telling funny tales involving me dad. Everyone around was in a real good mood, slapping each other on their backs, shaking hands, standing around drinking, smoking and having a right good laugh. I started to relax a little.

Dad came back and introduced me to a bloke called Raz. He'd been telling him about the time I'd got caught by a copper throwing stones at cars, but when he'd got hold of me, I wriggled away and all the copper had to take to the station was an old raggy coat. They all laughed at the idea of a copper putting handcuffs on an empty sleeve and reading the coat its rights.

I'd almost started to enjoy meself. Me dad had his arm slung across me shoulders and every now and then put me in a joke headlock and gave me a nuggy. It was the good old days again. I half expected me mam to come in and join in the fun. But then I remembered why we were there.

Maybe I could still save them. "Where are the badgers, Dad?" I asked. He glared at me and his mood instantly changed. He knew exactly what I was thinking. What could I do? There's no way I could stay and watch the baiting. Just the thought of it knocked me sick. Surely there had to be sommat I could do? If only I was as brave as Ahmed and James. Not that that did them any good though. Then I realised – they hadn't found Ahmed. Did they know there were two of them? I crossed me fingers in me pocket that Ahmed had escaped and got help. But who would he call? If he got James' dad they'd easily just mess him up. He'd be no good at all. If he called the police they'd arrest me dad, he'd go straight back to prison and I knew he'd rather do himself in than go back there. I didn't want that neither.

I made a decision. I'd been gutsy once already tonight, I was gunna do it again. I was gunna find the badgers and free them meself. If there were no badgers to fight, there was no crime. The badgers would be safe and me dad couldn't be done by the coppers.

I started joking around with me dad again, so he wouldn't suspect nowt. I recognised one of our neighbours, Old Macca. I'd got into a few scrapes with his son in the past when we'd gone nicking garden ornaments to sell. I brought him into the conversation and me dad was soon laughing remembering that I'd sold one of the ornaments back to the old lady I'd stolen it from 'cos she hadn't dared argue with me dad that it was hers.

"Dad where's the loo?" Me dad looked at me like he was trying to work out if I really needed it or was up to something. "Will yer come with me?" I asked, pretending I was a bit worried going on me own.

"No, go yerself, yer not a baby." he snapped at me, pointing towards the back of the building. "Through there out the back, there's some loos there."

I wandered off, trying to look like I wasn't in no rush. When I got outside, I found a tent. I could smell it before I could see it. There's no mistaking the stink of human crap. I decided that would be the perfect excuse if I was caught snooping around. I'd pretend I couldn't bear the smell and I was looking for a place to pee.

The shed that I'd just come out of was linked by some low fencing to another smaller shed. I was pretty certain that would be where I would find the badgers, and I could feel a faint tingle returning to me head. The low fencing was the same as the sides of the pit and made a kind of corridor. That must be how they got the badgers to enter the ring. A bit like the tunnel that footballers use to enter the stadium.

I ran up the corridor and through the door at the end. It smelt nice in here, no cigarette smoke, no human crap, just the smell of fresh straw. I glanced behind me, nobody had seen me. I sneaked a look over the first stall door, it was empty. Quickly, I looked over the second stall door. That was empty too. Just as I was thinking I'd got it wrong, I peeked over the third stall door and inside I saw a row of metal cages, each with an adult badger inside. There was no sign of the babies though. I crept up to the fourth stall, sneaked a look over the door and saw the cage with the babies in. In the last stall, I found James. Dead.

CHAPTER 15

* JAMES *

I could see little flickers in the blackness. Tiny sparks dancing and spinning, sometimes coming nearer, sometimes fading away. I watched them, confused. What were they? I tried to focus on one, but it made my head hurt too much then they disappeared and I felt myself fade away into the darkness.

The little dancing sparks returned. I tried focusing on one again. The pain was excruciating. Where was I? What had happened? Fuzzy memories started drifting back to me. I was in the tree den with Ahmed, then I was being chased through the woods. Why? I remembered a man punching me in the stomach then dragging me back through the woods. There was a Land Rover. And Greg. Greg Carlton. Why was he in the woods with a Land Rover? The badgers… he'd brought his dad to catch the badgers. I tried to sit up and my head swam again. I lay still.

Nearby, I thought I could hear Greg's grinding voice. I needed to get up, escape. I tried to move my head but it felt as heavy as concrete then the blackness washed back over me.

* GREG *

I just stood there staring at him. I couldn't believe it. Me stomach felt groggy and sweat dripped down me forehead. I turned away and spewed up.

When I looked back at him, I thought he'd changed position a bit. "James," I whispered. He moved. *Oh thank God!* He was in a bad way, his nose was a mess and he wasn't conscious, but he was alive. Had me dad done this? No, it must have been one of the others.

Just then, I heard voices heading towards the stinking tent. If I was gunna do sommat I'd have to be quick. The baiting was gunna start soon. I looked back at the badgers' stall. These ones weren't tied in sacks, they were just in metal cages. The men would grab one badger at a time by its tail and throw it into the pit with the dogs. *If all the badgers were loose though… maybe the men wouldn't dare go in the stall?*

I decided to open all the badgers' cages. It wasn't much of a plan. It bought time, but it wasn't gunna stop the fight happening. They'd bring the dogs in, sort the badgers back into cages and carry on. And me dad would know it was me. Also, there was a good chance the badgers would turn on me.

This worried me, I turned all the cages away from the stall door, and positioned meself between the cages and the door, ready to run for it.

Would I be able to talk to the badgers with me mind and let them know I wasn't the enemy? That I was helping them? It wasn't the best time to test my theory, but I had to give it a try, and make sure I was as close as possible to the stall door. There were six cages. I leaned over and opened the first one. The badger poked its nose forwards, sniffed and stayed where it was.

I'm here to help yer, I thought with as strong thought waves as I could manage. The badger ignored me and stayed in its cage. I opened the next cage. That badger stayed where it was as well. I opened each cage but every badger stayed where it was. Why weren't they escaping? Maybe I was wrong and they couldn't understand me thoughts. Then I remembered, when we used to watch Mr Blake, he'd come out of the sett and check for danger. If there was any doubt he'd reverse back in and stay where he was safe. They thought they were safe in their cages. To be fair, they weren't wrong. They had much more to fear once they got dragged out and into the fight pit. This wasn't gunna cause the badger baiters any problem at all. They'd just close the cage doors and carry on. I hadn't delayed the fight by more than about two minutes.

Me idea was that all the badgers would fight together as a team against the men, but the more I thought about it the dafter me idea seemed. Badgers stick together in family groups, but they're not team players like lions. In fact, I remembered James telling me that two boars from two different clans were likely to fight each other, so I might even have made things worse.

I stood there thinking. *What if I took away the pallets and bales supporting one of the tin sheets along the corridor, so if a badger pushed against it, it would just fall flat and it could escape? That would get one badger out. If it even pushed against the right one. Well one badger free was better than none.*

I left the stall door open and sneaked along the corridor. There was no-one around. Very quietly, I pulled the bales to one side. The hairs on me head and the back of me neck stood up. I felt like someone was watching me. I looked around but there was no-one there. I dragged the pallet away to the other side leaving the tin sheet barely balanced on its own. I still felt like someone was behind me, it was making me ears feel funny trying to hear a sound. I looked behind me again, but I couldn't see nowt. The moon had gone behind a cloud and everywhere was pitch black. I decided I better get back to the shed before I was missed.

As I headed back to the main shed, I heard me dad calling me. I peed up against the outside wall and shouted "Over 'ere, Dad."

He walked round, saw what I was doing and laughed. "Couldn't bear the smell, eh? I do the same." He peed up against the wall as well, and then we both walked back to the shed.

I was laughing at his jokes, but not listening to them, thinking what else I could do. I needed the badgers to all find that loose sheet together. Otherwise, it would be fixed after the first one escaped. The babies were still trapped in their cage too. And I needed to help James escape, but James was unconscious and unable to move himself. Nobody would be looking for James until the end of the night, after the fighting was finished. I would need to help the badgers first, then help James if I could.

It crossed me mind that I should call an ambulance for James, but the ambulance men would call the police. I couldn't risk it. Me dad was out on probation. If the police thought he had owt to do with this he'd be thrown back in prison without a second thought. I couldn't do that to him.

Just then, a big whooping set up among the men and they were all pushing and shoving each other trying to get closest to the ring. I tried to keep with me dad but we were getting pulled apart from each other. I saw his flat cap as he rode the wave to the front, and then me view was blocked by a huge wall of big square shoulders. It was impossible to push through, they were sturdier than steel. I stepped back and more men got in front of me. I wasn't gunna be able to see what was happening and I didn't wanna see. I let some other men push in front of me so that I was getting pushed further and further to the back without it being obvious that that's where I wanted to be.

Glancing towards the corridor that the badger would be coming out of, I could see men leaning over it and shouting but couldn't make out what was happening. I edged along the wall, wanting to see and not wanting to see what was happening.

They'd managed to separate one of the badgers

from the rest and two men were using a steel door to coral the badger down the corridor towards the ring and its violent death.

The corridor reminded me of a film I'd watched with me dad when all the prisoners on death row would watch one prisoner walking to the electric chair and they'd all chant, "Dead man walking." In the film they were hardened criminals and murderers, but even *they* had some pity for the bloke who was about to die. There was no pity from these men for the badger. They were jeering and shouting, excited that they were gunna see the badger get ripped to pieces.

Slowly, I slid into the shadows and as I did, me head started ringing. Not the tingle or even the pounding that I'd felt before. It was ringing like a million church bells were inside me head. And all over me skin I could feel the fear of that poor badger. I could feel the fear of all the badgers. I knew without a doubt that they were communicating their fear to me. I had to do sommat. I had to do it now.

Don't go into the ring, I screamed in me head. *Don't go into the ring!* But I knew the poor badger had no choice, the men were forcing it in. I had one last hope. One chance. I needed to communicate with the badgers and they needed to understand.

I stood straight upright, closed me eyes, clenched me fists, and thought as hard as I could. I pictured all the badgers running down the corridor together. I pictured them running up behind the two men with the steel door. I held me breath and put all me energy into me thoughts, picturing the scene again and again. Forcing the image to appear in me mind. A huge roar ran around the arena and I opened me eyes to see men chucking their dogs into the corridor. The badgers were all running down the corridor towards them. There were dogs and one badger on one side, the rest of the badgers on the other side, and the two men in the middle. Both men yelled and jumped over the side of the corridor.

I pictured the middle sheeting on the right falling down. I squeezed me eyes tight shut again and pictured the badgers barging at it and it falling, barging at it and it falling, barging at it and it falling. The crowd was screaming even more.

This time when I opened me eyes I saw panicked men running away from the corridor. The sheeting was on the floor and badgers and dogs were running everywhere. "Go to the woods," I screamed out loud, but I didn't need to. The badgers knew what they were doing now. They were out of the false man-made situation and back in more familiar territory. Some gutsy dogs still tried to attack them, but out in the open without a pit to contain the badgers, the dogs didn't have a chance anymore and the badgers quickly disappeared into the darkness.

All hell let loose. Men were turning on men, some dogs started fighting each other, some were fighting the men. Then I smelt smoke. The straw bales were on fire. A huge cry went up and everyone, me, the men, the dogs, all ran out the back to get away from the flames.

James! He was still unconscious in one of the stalls. And he was laid on a bed of straw. If the fire reached him he'd be a gonner.

I tried to run towards the stalls but a big bloke

held me back. "Gerrof me!" I yelled, but he wouldn't let go. He was behind me with his arms wrapped round me, pulling me backwards. I threw me head back and heard the crunch of his nose. He staggered backwards letting go of me and I sprinted round the side of the building to get in through the front.

There was a small window high up. I shoved some farm yard junk against it and climbed up. I could see James. He was sitting up but he still wasn't right. "James, the building's on fire, yer have to get out!" I screamed. He looked up at me confused, then he looked frightened… of me. "I'm here to help yer." He tried to stand up but he was real dizzy. I wriggled through and dropped down beside him. "'Ere, put yer arm over me shoulders, I'll help yer out." He obviously didn't trust me, but he had no choice, he couldn't stand on his own.

I grabbed the babies' cage in one hand and half supported, half dragged James down past the now empty badgers' stall towards the corridor. The fire was already racing towards us, I half lifted, half threw him and the cage over the little makeshift corridor wall and leaped over after them.

"Well done son, I'll take 'im from 'ere."

I looked up at me dad.

"Come on son, we need to get 'im in me Land Rover and to a hospital."

"Are you sure, Dad? Shouldn't we call an ambulance?"

"No son, they'll arrest me. I can't go back inside, no matter what. I'll drive 'im to the hospital meself and leave 'im in the car park, then I'll phone 'em to say where he is. Anonymous like. He'll be okay."

I helped me dad lift James into the footwell of the back seats of the Land Rover. James looked terrified but he didn't say nowt. He was still real woozy – I don't think he really understood what was going on.

I watched as me dad drove off down the farm track. Just as he was almost out of sight, I saw him turn left towards the quarry instead of right towards town and the hospital.

In that instant I knew what me dad was gunna do. I stood stock still and the panic rose up inside me. Me hands clenched into fists and sweat trickled down me face. It felt like I couldn't breathe properly and I started panting trying to get enough oxygen into me lungs. Me heart was pounding in me throat.

When me dad's dog, Bronx, had got too old to fight, me dad had shot him and threw him down a hole in the quarry. He'd come back laughing, saying you could easily get rid of dead bodies down there. The hole was so deep the smell would never reach the top. He'd said you could get away with murder.

CHAPTER 16

* JAMES *

Little sparks began to dance in front of my eyes again. I could hear lots of noise; men shouting, dogs barking, and I could smell smoke. Fire! I needed to get out. I tried to sit up. It felt like my brain was pounding against the inside of my skull, trying to burst out. I looked around me. If I moved my head too quickly, it pounded and I felt I was going to pass out again, but so long as I moved slowly I was okay. My vision was blurry but I could just about make out my surroundings. I was in some kind of stable, sitting on straw and there was an open stable door in front of me. To my horror, as I looked up, Greg Carlton's face appeared at a window high up on the wall.

I tried to get up and get away from Greg, but I couldn't make my legs work properly. The room was swimming round me and I fell back down. Greg jumped through the window and made me put my arm over his shoulders. I didn't trust him, but right now the smell of smoke was getting stronger and I couldn't get out without him. He carried me down some strange kind of walkway then threw me over the side. I landed on my back and as I looked up, I saw Greg's dad leaning over me.

Between them they threw me onto the floor of the back seats of the Land Rover and I knew then it was all over for me. I was too weak and dizzy to fight, I couldn't think straight to come up with a plan. It was over.

I lay there among the tools and rubbish and began to sob. How had this happened? How had my life come to this? I pictured my mum and dad crying at my funeral, then afterwards, sitting in my bedroom, looking at my bed and the pictures I'd drawn. I pictured my little sister growing up into a beautiful lady and not remembering that she ever had a big brother. Except my mum and dad wouldn't let her forget. They would read her the stories I'd written and show her photographs of me. They would always remember me, and when they died, they would be buried in the same grave as me. I shut my eyes and willed the blackness to come again, so I wouldn't have to feel whatever pain was about to end my life.

* GREG *

Just as me dad's Land Rover disappeared from view, I saw blue flashing lights and heard the welcome wail of sirens. Coppers! For the first time in me life I was actually glad to see bobbies. I sprinted towards them, waving me arms. The first cop car skidded to a stop. For a second I hesitated. I was about to dob me dad in to the cops. But he was about to kill a kid. I leaned through the window. "It's me dad. He's got James in his Land Rover and he's taking 'im to the quarry. I think he's gunna do 'im in."

"Jump in and show us the way," the copper shouted. I jumped in and saw Ahmed sat in the back. He must have got away and called them. He had a blanket wrapped round him and I realised he was sopping wet.

The copper spun the car round and we were bouncing up the track. "I don't think we'll make it, this car's too low to get up the path to the quarry. Yer need four-wheel-drive," I yelled.

"We can't go back and get one of the Land Rovers, there's no time, we'll just have to keep going forward. The helicopter should be with us any minute." Even as he said it, a huge light lit up the road ahead of us and we heard the low buzz of the police chopper.

* JAMES *

I lay there in the blackness, being thrown around over every bump. Then I remembered something Ahmed had told me his mum had taught him. If ever you're kidnapped, you have to make conversation with your kidnapper, make sure they know your name. It's much harder to kill someone once you've made some kind of connection with them and you're not just a 'body'.

"Mr Carlton?"

"Shut it!"

"Mr Carlton, it's me, James Taylor, I'm friends with your son, Greg."

"SHUT IT," he screamed.

I was scared, I didn't say anything for a little while, but then I realised I'd rather he was shouting at me than killing me, so I tried again. "Mr Carlton, Greg sometimes comes to play at my house. He's been learning about badgers and how they live."

Silence.

"He... Greg is good fun. I like him."

Silence.

"I... I hope he can come and play next weekend, he can stay over if he likes."

Mr Carlton spun round, his face purple with fury. "If you don't shut up, I'll knock yer head off yer shoulders. UNDERSTAND?"

I nodded.

Just then, we and the countryside around us was lit up by a huge bright light.

I must have still been a little muddled, because for a moment I thought it was an angel shining a light down from heaven for me. Then I heard a humming sound and realised it was the police helicopter.

"Mr Carlton, it's the police. Please, will you let me go now?"

"They're not gunna get yer." he snarled and shoved the vehicle into a lower gear forcing it to climb the side of the quarry more aggressively. "Once we reach the top, it'll be too late for everyone.

You, me, the police. Y'll all be too late."

And suddenly I understood. He'd rather die with me, than let me go and get caught.

In a panic, I sprang forward and yanked the steering wheel to face downhill. He shoved his big hand on my face and almost snapped my neck pushing me backwards, but I wouldn't let go. The Land Rover started bouncing faster and faster downhill, hitting rocks and throwing us around inside, like the dice in a desperate gambler's shaker. He grabbed my fingers and snapped them backwards off the steering wheel. I fell back to the floor and the hot pain of my broken fingers soared through me.

Mr Carlton swore as he regained control of the Land Rover and turned it uphill again. The sharpness of the pain in my fingers had cleared my head. I needed to make a plan.

I searched around on the floor and found a crowbar. Too long – I couldn't get it between the head rests to take a good swing at him. I found a knife and held it above my head ready to stab him through the top of his skull, but I just couldn't do it. I couldn't stick a blade into a living person's flesh. I rummaged around again and found a hessian sack. I grabbed it and flung it over Mr Carlton's head and the head rest, pulling with all my might, so he couldn't take it off. He took one hand off the steering wheel and tried to hit backwards at me, but he had no power at that angle. I pulled harder and he took both hands off the steering wheel to pull the sack off his face.

Without anyone steering it, the Land Rover started travelling downhill again picking up speed, bouncing out of control and heading towards rocks and trees. Suddenly, it tipped. There was a colossal crash. I felt a huge pain rip through my head, and all was black.

* GREG *

The cop car bounced and grinded along the path as far as it could, then crunched to a stop. The two coppers in the front jumped out and told me and Ahmed to stay in the car. A dog unit pulled up behind us and more coppers got out with big dogs barking and went running up the hill. I looked at Ahmed. His lips looked purple and he was shivering like mad. He was staring at me, probably trying to work out what I had to do with all this. I'd explain later, right now, I needed to know what was happening with me dad. And with James.

I jumped into the front of the cop car and out the door. Ahmed was still trying to open the back door. He'd work it out, I didn't have time to help him.

I ran up the hill. I could see the head lights of me dad's Land Rover zigzagging up and down the quarry wall. *James must be putting up a fight,* I thought.

Suddenly, there was a bang and the Land Rover was on its side. It wasn't moving anymore. Within seconds, the coppers swarmed over the Land Rover like black ants over a rotten piece of fruit. They dragged me dad out. He was kicking and screaming and shouting. It took a lot of coppers to get him down on the ground and cuffed. They even had to fasten his legs together.

He saw me and suddenly stopped shouting. The look he gave me turned me cold. It was pure hatred. Me dad hated me.

I stood there, staring at him. I'd done the wrong thing. I never should've told the coppers where me dad had gone. I never should've tried to help the badgers. I never should've made friends with the Taylors. I'd made everything go wrong. Now me dad was going back to prison and it was all me own fault.

A police woman tried to wrap a blanket round me. I shoved her away and ran back down the hill, past the empty cop cars. I was running blindly, crying and not even caring who saw me. I had no street-cred now, I'd just dobbed me dad in to the cops and you don't get worse than that. This was the worst night of me life.

As I ran down the track, I saw all the blue flashing lights outside The Sheds. The firemen were trying to put out the fire. I stood watching. I didn't know what to do with meself. Then I noticed a fireman carrying the cage that held Brock and Belinda. I ran up to them and shouted for them to hand the badgers to me. I knew the babies needed to get back to their sett as quickly as possible or they'd be rejected by their parents. Like me.

The fireman wouldn't let me take them. I was screaming at him, shouting, calling him all the names, trying to grab the cage from him. Another fireman came over and told me to calm down. I ran at him and kicked him but it hardly hurt him with all the fire protective gear he was wearing. Then a copper started on me. They always have to join in when someone's having a bad time. He threatened to throw me in the back of the police van. As if I cared. The first fireman told me he'd already called for the RSPCA, so I should let the professionals handle it, but I knew they wouldn't know which sett the badgers were from. I kept screaming this at them but they wouldn't listen and in the end, the coppers threw me in the back of the van anyway to 'calm down'.

The back of a police van is not somewhere that makes you feel calm. It's the last place you'd wanna be if you were feeling angry. First of all, everything is bright white so it hurts your eyes. Secondly, it's a CAGE. I looked at the cage walls and I thought about the babies trapped in their cage. I thought about me dad and how he hated me and the prison cage they would throw him in. I thought about the babies and how their parents would probably not recognise them and might even try to kill them. I wished me dad would kill me. I was sick of this life.

* * *

CHAPTER 17

* JAMES *

When I woke up in hospital, it took me a while to realise where I was. I kept having panic attacks because I thought I was back in the stable with fire all around me, or back in the Land Rover with a lunatic at the wheel. Mum was there the whole time to calm me down each time I woke up.

I kept screaming Greg's name. I hated him. Hated him to the pit of my stomach for everything. For betraying the badgers, for being a badger baiter, for throwing me into the Land Rover, for wanting me dead. The hate for him was so strong it made me retch up bile.

When I was well enough, a policeman visited me in hospital to take my statement.

What he told me shocked me to the core. I couldn't believe it at first. I thought they'd got it all wrong. I thought that Greg must have lied to them to get out of trouble, but the policeman assured me it all checked out.

Not only had Greg tried to save the badgers, he'd tried to save me as well. Greg had managed to save all the adults in our clan. Then he'd released all the other badgers at The Sheds, although it was a little unclear how he'd managed to help them all escape outside. I think they must have been running away from the fire.

After the policeman had gone, I felt terribly guilty. I lay there for a long time, staring up at the ceiling, lost in thought. Thinking about Greg and why he'd done what he'd done. His dad would go to prison now. I don't think I could ever tell on my dad if it meant he would go to prison. But then my dad would never do what Greg's dad had done, so I couldn't really imagine myself in his position. I started to feel sorry for Greg. When I hadn't known him, I'd hated him. Then, when he'd started coming round ours, I'd grown to quite like him, but the minute everything had gone wrong, I'd assumed the worst and gone straight back to hating him. What sort of a life must he have? His dad in and out of prison, everyone assuming him to be as bad as his dad. What if he wasn't bad? Not deep inside. What must it be like to grow up in a family like that? With everyone expecting the worst of you – even those who know you. I didn't know how he must feel. I just couldn't imagine it.

I decided as soon as I was out of hospital that I would find a way to make it up to Greg. I would start by inviting him to mine and Ahmed's sleep-overs. When Ahmed came over he had an even better idea.

"We all love staying in the tree den – why don't we all go camping?"

* GREG *

My life has changed so much in two weeks. For starters, I don't have to live at home anymore. I've moved in to me Uncle Kev's properly instead of just odd weekends here and there. Me little brother still lives with me mam, but he comes to see me at me

Uncle Kev's. He says our mam's trying to stop drinking and she's cleaned the house up. I hope she does for Kyle's sake, but I won't be going back there. Me mam and Kyle go and visit Dad in prison but I haven't gone with them. Dad won't wanna see me and I don't wanna see him.

A few days after everything happened, I got a surprise knock at me Uncle Kev's door. It was Mr and Mrs Taylor, James and Ahmed. They'd come to see how I was and they called me a hero. Haha! Get that – a hero. James and Ahmed were the real heroes. I'd frozen to the spot when I first saw the badger baiters, it was James and Ahmed who threw themselves into Rambo-mode. Anyway, they took me out for a meal which was real nice of them and Mrs Taylor kept making a real big fuss of me and crying and saying I'd saved James' life. I felt a bit guilty 'cos I didn't deserve all their praise. I'd helped Dad load James into the Land Rover, but Mrs Taylor wouldn't hear nowt about that and just kept telling me I did the right thing when it counted.

Mrs Taylor insisted I come round the next day because her and Mr Taylor had a surprise for us all.

We were all sat round the tiny kitchen table eating Mr Taylor's flat, soggy cupcakes and swilling them down with over-stewed tea. Mrs Taylor had Rosie sat on her knee and kept grinning at Mr Taylor, who kept grinning back at her. I could see Ahmed was dying to ask but it was James who gave in first. "Mum, Dad, what's the surprise? What is it?"

"Well," Mr Taylor began in a stern voice, "it would seem to me, that none of you three boys are very good at staying in your beds when you're supposed to. Mrs Taylor and I go to sleep thinking James is tucked up safely in his bed, with Ahmed safely tucked up on the camper bed beside him and Greg is safely tucked up in his own bed at home."

"In reality," Mrs Taylor continued, "it would appear that on more than one occasion, all three of you boys have sneaked outside to sleep under the stars."

We all went silent. This wasn't going as well as I'd hoped. I wasn't sure how much the police had told them, one of the coppers had wheedled it out of me that I was in the woods more than I was at home and she got me a social worker. I wasn't too bothered though 'cos it was the social worker who arranged for me to move in at Uncle Kev's. Still, I didn't want Mr Taylor thinking badly of me.

Mr Taylor looked at us all. "It's almost the summer holidays. How can we trust you to stay indoors? In fact, I'll re-phrase that. How can we *expect* you to stay indoors?"

James and Ahmed and I looked at each other, we weren't sure where he was going with this.

"So ... we're changing our expectations. We're *expecting* you all to sleep outdoors, because... we're all going camping."

I couldn't believe it. We were *all* going camping. I just couldn't believe me luck. The three of us just sat there stunned, grinning like idiots. *Flash!* Mrs Taylor had taken a picture of us with our stupid grins. Great!

Ahmed and James jumped up and started dancing round the kitchen whooping and yelling. Then Mr and Mrs Taylor jumped up and joined in.

Andrew started barking and jumping up and down with them. They were making a massive noise. I just sat there, watching them and laughing, still with me idiot grin on me face. They're all bonkers the lot of them – in a good way.

Eventually, everyone calmed down enough to sit back down and start asking Mr and Mrs Taylor where were we going? When were we going? How long for?

In the middle of the excitement, there was a knock at the door. Mr Taylor went to answer it and came back to the kitchen. Behind him was a woman from the RSPCA. She had bad news. Belinda and Brock couldn't go back to their own clan so they had to be fostered until they were old enough to be released to a new site. That brought me back down. Even though I'd expected it, I was gutted that the lovely family had been broken up. Belinda and Brock hadn't done nowt wrong, but now they'd been rejected by their parents. Just like me.

The woman looked at us all looking miserable. "The badgers have been placed with a farmer who helps us to foster badger cubs when they have become separated from their parents for whatever reason. We have told him about the three of you and he has asked if you would like to help him take care of them. He's part of a group who specialise in badger protection."

I had no idea that kind of thing existed. James whooped and jumped in the air. Then he ran upstairs and came back down with a diary. Apparently, he had been keeping a diary on the badgers all this time. What a geek. Haha! But he's alright even if he is a geek.

I was real happy about being able to see Belinda and Brock again. Mr Taylor said he'd take us each evening to help the farmer. Nobody needed to warn us to keep the address top secret. There was no way we were letting anyone find out where these poor babies were hiding out. The RSPCA woman said we wouldn't be allowed to touch the badgers 'cos we couldn't risk them trusting humans. I got that. But we'd be able to watch them playing in their pen and we'd clean their bedding out like their mam used to and the farmer would let us prepare their food.

That night we all piled into Mr Taylor's car and drove for about half an hour before we reached the farm.

The farmer introduced himself as Phil and showed us where he was keeping the badgers. He was an odd-looking fella. You could tell he thought more about the animals than he did himself. He was massive with dirty, shaggy hair. He looked like he needed a good scrub and a new set of clothes, but you could see by his eyes that he was harmless and kind. He talked real quiet and gentle-like.

Leading us down a corridor in a big barn, he turned to us and put his hand to his lips for us to be silent. Then he pointed over a steel wall. As we looked over, we saw the back end of Brock and Belinda as they scuttled back into their artificial den – they'd seen us first. Phil took us down to the feed room and showed us how to weigh out their food. They were on dog food with dead chicks thrown on top. Yuck! We pushed it through a little service hatch for them and then went back to the feed room where Phil had set up CCTV cameras to watch them feeding. He said we had to keep an eye on them 'cos Brock would try to take all the food, but Belinda would put up a good struggle and barge him out the way to get enough for herself. That didn't surprise us, we knew she could look after herself alright.

I went home happy that night. I felt real good about saving the badgers and now helping to look after them. I didn't tell Uncle Kev what I was doing 'cos I knew he wouldn't understand. He'd just think I was soft. But it didn't matter. I was dead happy and I fell asleep dreaming about badgers and camping.

I guess I wouldn't have slept so well if I'd known what was gunna happen when we went camping, but I'll tell you about that another time. For now, life was quiet. Life was good.

AFTERWORD

Dear Readers,

I'm sure Greg, James and Ahmed will continue to help the local badger protection group long after Brock and Belinda have been released back into the wild. Would you also like to help protect badgers and save them from wildlife crime?

You can find your local Badger Trust support group or find other ways to help, such as raising money for donations by visiting their website:

www.badgertrust.org.uk

Important note to all children. If, you feel unsafe or in danger, you can call the police.
In the United Kingdom (that's England, Scotland, Wales and Northern Ireland) you can also phone Childline on 0800 1111

TEST YOUR KNOWLEDGE

What do you know about badgers? After reading this story and researching on the Badger Trust website, you may be surprised at just how much you have learned about badgers.

Answer True or False (Answers are upside down at the end)

1) Badgers live underground in setts. They have one main sett and then several other smaller setts within their area.

2) Badgers are aggressive and will attack for no reason.

3) Setts can be handed down through the generations so a badger sett can be over 100 years old.

4) Badgers are dirty and are covered in their own faeces.

5) Badgers leave little pooh piles called "latrines" to mark the perimeter of their territory and warn other badgers to stay out.

6) A group of badgers living together is called a clan.

7) Badgers are protected. It is illegal to interfere with a badger or its sett and you can be fined or even sent to prison.

8) Badgers are carnivores so they only eat meat.

9) Badgers, separated from their families cannot be returned if too much time has passed and their scent has changed.

10) Badgers are wild animals and should never be approached.

11) Badgers become less active in winter but do not hibernate.

12) Badgers are mostly nocturnal.

13) Regardless of when the badgers mate, the cubs will always be born around February.

14) Badgers make great pets.

15) Badgers cannot feel emotions, therefore they do not care for each other or play together or experience fear or suffering.

		8)	F
15)	F	7)	T
14)	F	6)	T
13)	T	5)	T
12)	T	4)	F
11)	T	3)	T
10)	T	2)	F
9)	T	1)	T

ABOUT THE AUTHOR

Rachel Coverdale was born and bred in the beautiful North Yorkshire countryside in North East England. Raised with copious amounts of animals, and without the distraction of a modern TV set, she turned to books and her own imagination for entertainment. Animals were and still are a huge part of her life and inevitably they made their way into her stories. She is keen to promote animal welfare and wishes to raise awareness about the vulnerability of British wildlife, particularly badgers.

As an adult, Rachel has worked with many troubled children and is passionate about highlighting their plights and encouraging people to see the damaged child hiding behind the poor behaviour.

Rachel also writes books for younger children. Believing strongly in fresh air, nature and outdoor play to give children a sense of fun and freedom, she uses her books to encourage children to venture into the countryside.

Contact details:
https://www.rachelcoverdale.com
https://www.facebook.com/rachellouisecoverdale/
https://twitter.com/RLCoverdale
https://www.instagram.com/rachellouisecoverdale/
email: rachelcoverdale.author@hotmail.com

If you would like to know about future books I will be writing, please join the mailing list on my website:
https://www.rachelcoverdale.com

Teacher resources available.

Printed in Great Britain
by Amazon